PRAISE FOR
WHEN TOMORROW BURNS

"Captivatingly thoughtful, utterly unforgettable, and singularly brilliant. Part probing exploration of prophecy, part searing call to action, part pitch-perfect rendering of middle school dynamics—all woven into a masterful tapestry. I haven't stopped thinking about it since I read it. Tae Keller is one of my absolute favorite writers, and this just might be her best work yet."

—**JASMINE WARGA**, #1 *New York Times* bestselling and Newbery Honor–winning author

"Another unforgettable novel from one of my favorite authors. I loved Nomi, Arthur, and Vi. I have a prophecy that readers will love them, too."

—**ERIN ENTRADA KELLY**, two-time Newbery Medalist and National Book Award finalist

"In our uncertain world, Tae Keller's tender and powerful novel explores the impact of stories, friendship, and ultimately, hope."

—**LISA YEE**, Newbery Honor winner and National Book Award finalist

"Tae Keller hopes *When Tomorrow Burns* will offer readers 'a resting place for big feelings and big questions,' and wow, does it ever. Keller's writing brims with empathy and compassion as her characters endure excruciating embarrassments, messy friendships, and the myriad complications of growing up in the twenty-first century. A story as lovely as the mystery woven throughout it, *When Tomorrow Burns* will be a spark in the dark for young readers everywhere."

—**MEGAN E. FREEMAN**, *New York Times* bestselling author

"*When Tomorrow Burns* is for anyone who's ever sensed a whisper of magic in a tree, a book, a friendship—or anyone who wants to. I loved it."

—**ELANA K. ARNOLD**, National Book Award finalist and Printz Honor–winning author

ALSO BY TAE KELLER

The Science of Breakable Things
When You Trap a Tiger
Jennifer Chan Is Not Alone

The Mihi Ever After Series

We Carry the Sun

WHEN TOMORROW BURNS

TAE KELLER

RANDOM HOUSE 🏠 NEW YORK

Random House Books for Young Readers
An imprint of Random House Children's Books
A division of Penguin Random House LLC
1745 Broadway, New York, NY 10019
penguinrandomhouse.com
rhcbooks.com

Text copyright © 2026 by Tae Keller
Jacket art copyright © 2026 by Cornelia Li
Interior tree art copyright © 2026 by Megan Shortt

Penguin Random House values and supports copyright. Copyright fuels creativity, encourages diverse voices, promotes free speech, and creates a vibrant culture. Thank you for buying an authorized edition of this book and for complying with copyright laws by not reproducing, scanning, or distributing any part of it in any form without permission. You are supporting writers and allowing Penguin Random House to continue to publish books for every reader. Please note that no part of this book may be used or reproduced in any manner for the purpose of training artificial intelligence technologies or systems.

Random House and the colophon are registered trademarks of Penguin Random House LLC.

Library of Congress Cataloging-in-Publication Data
Names: Keller, Tae author
Title: When tomorrow burns / Tae Keller.
Description: First edition. | New York: Random House, 2026. |
Audience: Ages 8–12 years | Summary: "Three former friends reunite to find a book that could save their lives and friendship"—Provided by publisher.
Identifiers: LCCN 2025005018 (print) | LCCN 2025005019 (ebook) | ISBN 978-0-593-48558-3 (hardcover) | ISBN 978-0-593-48559-0 (lib. bdg.) | ISBN 978-0-593-48560-6 (ebook)
Subjects: CYAC: Friendship—Fiction | Prophecies—Fiction | Fate and fatalism—Fiction | Middle schools—Fiction | Schools—Fiction | LCGFT: Novels
Classification: LCC PZ7.1.K418 Wh 2026 (print) | LCC PZ7.1.K418 (ebook)

Watercolor worn old paper by Masha_tolk_art/stock.adobe.com and watercolor flame by Alexandra/stock.adobe.com.

The text of this book is set in 12-point Bembo MT Pro.

Manufactured in the United States of America
1st Printing

The authorized representative in the EU for product safety and compliance is Penguin Random House Ireland, Morrison Chambers, 32 Nassau Street, Dublin D02 YH68, Ireland, https://eu-contact.penguin.ie.

Random House Children's Books supports the First Amendment and celebrates the right to read.

To the people I love in Seattle—

Who advocate for clean energy, sustainability, affordable housing, education, books, medical care, justice, laughter, and joy. To the Saturday-morning volunteers, writers, artists, gardeners, teachers, thinkers, and dreamers—

Thank you for showing me what it means to plant seeds and help them grow.

ONCE, THERE WAS A TREE.

For two hundred years there was a tree, there was a tree, there was a tree.

Until a tree fell in a forest—and then there was a book.

PART I

*Pink and gray both on one day.
The world has tipped, you have no say.*

NOMI

UNTIL SEPTEMBER 5TH, THE DAY THE GRAY ROLLED IN and choked Seattle's sky with ash, Nomi had almost forgotten about the prophecy.

To be clear, Nomi was not the kind of kid who believed in prophecies. She didn't suspect things. She didn't have hunches. She believed in things that could be proven with evidence, cold and hard as fact.

And on that morning, September 5th, day of the gray, prophetic, et cetera, et cetera, she was thinking of facts.

Fact: She'd ridden the city bus to school alone that morning, which meant Arthur was either sleeping, or sick, or faking sick—not that she cared, because she was definitively not friends with Arthur.

Fact: The route from her apartment to school contained four billboards. Two of them were for some kind of insurance. One was a phone number to speak to Jesus. And the last was a digital billboard outside an Amazon building. The exact word or phrase changed every few weeks, but it was always vague and didn't seem to advertise anything in particular.

For the past two weeks, ever since seventh grade started, it had said BREATHE, which had felt, before today, like an unnecessary reminder, and now felt moderately tragic, considering the sky was filled with smoke.

Fact: Nomi got off the bus to find Violet, as usual, scrolling through her phone, as usual, sitting under the old oak tree, as usual, the same one they'd sat under since first grade. And then Nomi actually *did* cease to breathe, because Violet looked different—and change always made Nomi's heart skip a step.

Walking up to Violet, she searched for breath, searched for words. "Do you have a piano recital?" she finally asked, attempting to lighten her voice as she gestured to her best friend's outfit.

Violet didn't answer right away, but that was normal for her. Unlike Nomi, Violet always thought things through about six times before she spoke. It was what made them a good pair.

Violet's lips quirked like she was trying not to laugh, and she slid her phone into her backpack. (Normally she would've slid it into her pocket, but she couldn't, considering she'd swapped her everyday jeans for a pocketless pink skirt.) "It's been over a year since I played piano. You know that."

"But then . . . why . . ." Nomi could not say, *Why do you look so different?* so she said, ". . . the pink?"

"No reason." Violet tucked a strand of shiny black hair behind her ear and smoothed her hand over her outfit, like she was reminding herself it was there. Pink striped skirt, pink shirt—no, pink *blouse*—pink headband, pink wedge heels. "Haven't you ever changed something just because?"

Nomi had been best friends with Violet long enough to develop a sixth sense. She knew when Violet was about to catch a cold. She knew when Violet was annoyed with her little sister, Blue. And she always, always knew when Violet was lying.

Nomi gave Violet a look.

"I'm not lying," Violet lied. "There's nothing to worry about."

And that was when Nomi remembered the prophecy.

She hadn't thought about it in years, but now it blotted her mind like light on night-soaked retinas. It was all she could think about.

She grabbed Violet's wrist, concern over a new outfit blooming into something larger. "The book said this would happen."

For a few seconds, the only expression on Violet's face was confusion. Then her eyes widened. "Nomi. Absolutely not—"

But Nomi wasn't listening.

What were the chances Violet would trade in her jeans and Target T-shirts the exact same day the wildfires started? Statistically unlikely! Slim to none! Which meant it couldn't be a coincidence.

The final prophecy was coming true. Nomi didn't suspect it. She knew it.

Fact.

NOMI

YEARS AGO, IN THE MUSEUM OF LOST AND FOUND, Nomi, Violet, and Arthur had discovered a book that told the future.

Of course, they hadn't known that it told the future. Not at first.

Arthur had said, *Ugh, poetry.* And Violet had said, *An old diary. That's nice.*

But Nomi had been captivated. It was her favorite thing she'd ever seen in the museum.

One of Arthur's dads, Anthony, had started the museum by collecting pieces of artwork abandoned on the street—near trash cans, on stoops, in piles of recycling.

"It's like 'one person's trash is another person's treasure,'" Nomi's mom had said, "but Anthony made it literal."

Lots of people wanted their art to be treasured, as it turned out, because soon enough artists started leaving paintings, sculptures, and poems by the gallery doors, like blanketed babies by a firehouse. The museum grew until it took over the whole first floor of Arthur's apartment, and it became one of the most popular galleries in downtown Seattle.

To be perfectly honest, Nomi had decided a long time ago that she didn't *get* art, and though Arthur's dads tried to explain it (*Art is about becoming,* Anthony always said), the museum gave Nomi the strangest, most uncomfortable feeling. Because the artists could be anybody. She could pass them on the street and have no idea, and that thought gave her a spindly-tingling sensation.

But the book—

It was Arthur who'd pulled it off the shelf. "Look what showed up last night," he'd said. Back then, he was always showing them things, eager and nervous like he cared what they thought.

They were buzzing with energy. Anything would've excited Nomi, probably.

But the book was another level.

There was something about it. Maybe it was the old leather binding and the crinkly, browned paper that said, *This is old, like, ancient.* Maybe it was the way the scrawled entries were written in faded blue ink, or the way the handwriting was just barely legible, which made each line feel like a puzzle, or the way the little poems and phrases had the lilt and tilt of fantastical prophecies.

She knew it was silly, but as she read them, the hairs on her neck stood up. She wouldn't call it magic—she would *never*—but there was something there that she couldn't quite describe.

And then the little poems started coming true.

In pea-green pockets, promises of tomorrow.

Nomi found an old pop quiz in her green coat, and the next day their teacher surprised them with another one.

When leaves flutter, too high to climb, too far to fall.

Violet tried to help her dad clean the gutters in the fall, and then fell off the ladder, spraining her ankle.

A taste of something new, and something blue.

Arthur's other dad, Brian, arrived at dinner one night with a brand-new flavor of ice cream: blue bubble gum.

These might've seemed like coincidences if they hadn't happened so often, with the prophecies coming true in order, one after the other, reliable and undeniable.

Before the book, Nomi's life had been unpredictable. Her mom had gotten laid off, making money troubles even more troubling. Then they'd had to move to a smaller apartment. And then the pandemic had shut the world down.

After the book, though, the future became something she could plan for. It became safe. Trustworthy.

Until that final page.

ARTHUR

IN THEORY, ARTHUR TOOK THE BUS TO AND FROM school. But in reality, come on.

The bus required him to wake a whole forty minutes earlier, and riding the bus with Nomi was, well, awkward.

His phone alarm sounded for the eighth time, and he half cracked an eye as he fumbled for the snooze button.

A series of preprogrammed reminders from his dads filled his screen.

> DON'T YOU DARE PRESS THE SNOOZE BUTTON!!! —Danthony

> Waking up on time was part of the agreement when we got you this phone. You signed a binding contract. —Abba

> YOU OWE US YOUR FIRSTBORN CHILD IF YOU PRESS SNOOZE AGAIN.
> —Danthony (the cool one)

> Anthony, don't pressure him for grandkids. He's twelve.
> —Abba, the Cool but *Responsible* One

> (chanting) GRANDKIDS! GRANDKIDS! (whispering) In twenty years. If you so choose. —Danthony, also a v. responsible dad

Arthur groaned and flipped his phone face down. Most of the time, he didn't mind his dads' antics. But at 6:27 a.m.? No thank you.

"Good morning, rise and shine, all that good stuff." Danthony cracked Arthur's bedroom door open and leaned against the doorframe. When Arthur was little, his dads had cycled through different names. Brian was always Abba, but Anthony tried Pops, then Daddy, then Dad. It was Danthony, though—a joke that started as Dad-Anthony—that had stuck.

He sipped a mug of steaming coffee, though it was still

too hot outside for that. "The bus leaves in three minutes, as I'm sure you're aware."

Abba was always busy with work stuff at the crack of dawn, and this past year, the Museum of Lost and Found had gotten major media attention, which meant Danthony often had morning calls with fancy East Coast curators.

Which meant: bus for Arthur.

Arthur grunted something, attempting to communicate the general sense of *I'm sleeping* without bothering to form actual human words.

"However." His dad ran a hand through his hair. It was the same color as Arthur's, somewhere between blond and brown, like it couldn't decide. "I don't have any meetings this morning, so out of the goodness of my heart, I will drive you, because I am a kind, generous father."

Arthur smashed a pillow over his face. "Why do I have to get up before the sun?"

"Blame institutionalized capitalism and American workism," Danthony said. "Not me."

Arthur groaned. 6:29 a.m. *No thank you.*

"Get ready to greet the day!" his dad said, hesitating before adding, "And wear a mask. Smoke's bad today."

Arthur contemplated faking a life-threatening illness. Lucas had gotten appendicitis last year, which he said hurt like his insides were on fire, but it had gotten him out of a math test and he hadn't even had to retake it.

No, no hope of appendicitis.

He dragged himself out of bed, ready to greet the day.

He'd been ready to greet the day, but he hadn't been ready to greet *Nomi*.

Yet there she was.

Arthur had just gotten out of his car at the drop-off, and his dad had barely driven away before Nomi marched up, dragging Violet along by the wrist.

Arthur normally spent his mornings by the lockers with Lucas and the other cross-country guys, and Nomi and Violet sat under the oak tree by the drop-off. Arthur *thought* they'd had an unspoken agreement to avoid each other at school—but apparently Nomi didn't care about breaking it.

She stood in front of him, blocking his path. The thing about Nomi was she had so much energy. Her green eyes burned. Her freckles nearly leapt off her pale cheeks. Her brown hair puffed up around her face, like it was demanding your attention.

"We have to prevent complete and utter annihilation," she announced, as if that were not a bizarre thing to say to someone you barely spoke to.

Arthur opened his mouth. Closed it. Opened it. Being around Nomi did this to him. She just moved so *fast*. She had so much to *say*. She was top-scholarship-level smart, and it showed. "Hi?"

Violet gave a half-hearted wave with her non-Nomi-ed

hand. She looked different, for reasons Arthur couldn't put a finger on. A haircut? Maybe. Was he supposed to mention it? But what if she *hadn't* gotten a haircut?

Too much time had passed. Now he was staring.

Violet didn't seem to notice. "That's not what the book said," she told Nomi. "You're overdramatizing."

"I'm *paraphrasing*," Nomi corrected. "Violet, listen! 'How do you turn a girl to flame?' And 'You'll never be the same.' That sounds pretty annihilating to me."

Arthur frowned. The phrases sounded familiar, but he couldn't place them.

Nomi sighed. She was always sighing at him like she was waiting for him to catch up. "The *book*, Arthur. Remember the book?"

Oh. The book.

Arthur already had a headache, and the conversation had barely started. When Nomi got like this, Violet used to call it Level 5 Nomi. "The book of poetry?"

"Of *prophecy*. The one you, me, and Violet found. Pea-green pockets. Burning canopies. Et cetera."

She didn't need to remind him. Poetry, prophecy, whatever—of course he remembered that book.

"Oh, I forgot to mention," Violet said, mostly to Nomi, all forced casual, "it's Vi now."

Nomi's brow pinched. "What's vie?"

"Me. I'm Vi."

Nomi stared at her best friend. "Why?"

A look passed between the girls, a whole silent

conversation—and not a pleasant one. A new nickname didn't seem like a big deal to Arthur, but he wasn't about to say that. He sensed conflict brewing, which he didn't get involved with, as a general rule.

"Just because," Vi said quietly, like she didn't want Arthur to hear. Arthur felt, very strongly, like he shouldn't be there.

When Nomi didn't respond, Vi murmured, "Violet's just too much."

Nomi hesitated, then shook her head and refocused her megawatt attention onto Arthur.

"Well, anyway." Her eyes bored into him with an intensity that made the backs of his knees turn to mud. "We need to talk to Anthony."

"My dad?" Arthur could think of nothing worse than bringing these girls home to talk to his dad. His parents had been dramatically heartbroken when Arthur stopped hanging out with them. (*Bereft,* Danthony had announced. Abba had added, *Girls and boys* can *be friends, you know. But we understand.*) It didn't have to be such a big deal, in Arthur's opinion. "Why do you need to talk to him?"

"Because," Nomi said, like the answer was obvious, "we need to find the sequel. Part two. If the first book promises disaster, then the second book will tell us how to fix it."

Arthur blinked. "And you're gonna find the sequel . . . how?"

"One: Find out who wrote the book. Two: Track them down. Three: Ask them where the sequel is. Four: Get the second book. Five: Prevent annihilation."

Arthur could have told her that was impossible—everything in the Museum of Lost and Found came in anonymously—but he'd known Nomi long enough to know that telling her something was impossible just made her more determined. "You can visit the museum tomorrow." He shrugged. "Since I won't be there."

Nomi frowned, and Arthur realized that that last bit had come out harsh. Which was annoying, because he hadn't meant it to be harsh. He was just telling her so she wouldn't feel awkward, since obviously it would be awkward if he was there. Whatever. He was trying to be nice. "I'll be at my cross-country meet."

The meet ended pretty early in the day, but he'd make plans with Lucas or something. At the very least he'd hide upstairs in his bedroom so he wouldn't have to see them.

Nomi nodded, and when their eyes met, Arthur's stomach squeezed in that familiar way. He couldn't tell if he hated the feeling or wanted more of it.

The first bell saved him.

"Sorry," Vi said, "I have to get to math. Don't want Mr. Romero to be mad."

It sounded like an excuse, considering Arthur had never seen Mr. Romero get mad, but Vi hurried away, leaving Arthur and Nomi standing under the tree.

He had to get away.

The poem, the prophecy, *whatever*, had predicted exactly this feeling:

A friendship ends with a crush. Too much.

They hadn't known what that meant, or who that prophecy would affect, until last summer, the night of Vi's final piano recital. Arthur and Nomi had attended with their parents, like they always did, and Arthur sat next to Nomi, like he always did, but when the lights went down, Arthur suddenly became very aware that Nomi's knee was approximately six inches from his own. And also that the way she was wearing her hair was kinda nice.

And everything inside him went, *Oh no.*

He kept hoping things would return to normal when the lights came on, but they didn't. His whole world shifted, and though he tried to push it back into place, it was too late. He couldn't stop staring at Nomi. And thinking about her. And his words went un-word-shaped around her, and it was pretty much the worst thing ever.

So he let the friendship drift, and even though he missed her and Vi sometimes, even though he felt a little guilty about it, come on. He didn't want to be involved with that. A crush on Nomi was, in fact, way too much.

Nomi hadn't seemed to notice then that his world was imploding, and she wasn't paying much attention to him now, either.

A crease formed between her brows as she watched Vi walk away. "She's got a secret," Nomi murmured, more to herself than to Arthur.

And Arthur didn't want to get involved, but if he did, he would have said, *Everyone does.*

VI

SOMETIMES, IN THE PRIVACY OF HER THOUGHTS, VI liked to imagine that each secret had a flavor. What would this one taste like? A little bitter, probably, but . . . almost addictive. Like a fresh orange peel.

She dragged her thumb over her phone, letting the school day slide from her mind as she returned to her latest secret. It had been an exhausting day, with all Nomi's talk of annihilation, so Vi had climbed right into bed as soon as she got home, pulling the sheets up to her chin, curling around her phone.

The mix of clothing ads, vacation photos, and wildfire news on her Instagram feed was jarring as she scrolled—it was part of the reason she'd barely used the app before.

In fact, she'd forgotten she even had an account until two days ago, when she'd googled herself on a whim and made an awful discovery. *Violet Kim.* The first dozen hits or so were other Violets, other Kims, mostly old Korean ladies.

But then she'd found it, an old blog called *Raising Wildflowers*, which led to a newer Instagram account, which led to Vi's stomach clawing up her chest and into her esophagus.

Because there, photo after perfectly framed photo, were Vi and her sister, Blue. Or, rather, Violet and Bluebell.

Her mother didn't use their names on Instagram the way she had on the blog, but that didn't change much. It was still Violet's face. Still her stories.

There was Violet at five, red-faced and tearstained, holding a bloody little piece of white. *First tooth!* her mother had written. *And what a debacle it was . . .*

Three whole paragraphs dedicated to Violet losing her first tooth: how she'd slipped, rammed into a wall, found her mouth full of blood, thought she was dying, and then peed her pants.

Six thousand likes! Eight hundred comments!

And there was Violet again, years later, in a velvet red dress at her piano recital. She remembered that recital, the last one her grandmother had been alive for. Vi had only played because of her. Her grandmother loved piano, insisted that the music ran in the family (skipping Vi's dad, but sure).

My little flower hates dressing up, the caption read, *(almost as much as she hates practicing piano)! Tell me—do you force your kiddos to follow through on their extracurriculars (not cheap, btw!) or do you cave to their cries of "don't make me go!"*

Vi refreshed the page and found a new photo, posted five minutes ago.

Violet again, just last week, sitting at the kitchen table with a box of cereal propped in front of her, laughing at something she could no longer remember. *My little flower's growing up. She's my baby, but I can already see the woman she'll become. Tell me, mamas, how do you do it? How do you let them go when all you want to do is squeeze them close? (And with this organic cereal, she's growing far too fast!) #ad*

Vi stared at that photo, palms going slick as the likes and emoji-filled comments rolled in. Parents poured their hearts out, talking about their own "mama journeys."

A comment at the top had already gained twenty-two likes. *Is it weird that I'm a little verklempt, too? I've been following you since the blog. Feels like I watched her grow up.*

Vi closed the app, her heart beating as if something were chasing her.

It wasn't like she was unaware of her mom's camera. Her mom liked taking photos, but so did lots of people. Vi didn't care when she saw her face all over her mom's phone.

But seeing it online was different. All those people, all those likes, all those opinions . . . they made Vi feel unreal. Like an impostor in her own skin. Like she might not even be there—

A smoke alarm blared outside her room, dragging her back to her body, demanding drop-everything panic, but Vi didn't leave her bed.

Instead she wrapped her duvet tighter and burrowed deeper into her phone.

Her mother's footsteps thundered down the hallway outside. *"Bluebell!"*

Three, two, one . . .

The alarm stopped. For the fourth time this week.

Vi closed her eyes in relief, her ears ringing with quiet.

And then her little sister's voice: "Upstairs hallway: check! Next up . . ."

Three, two—

Vi's door banged open and Blue burst in, waving a broom over her head. She wore a rainbow shirt under purple overalls, along with her plastic green rain hat, which she donned every day, regardless of the weather. The world's most colorful, and most prepared, seven-year-old. "Fire-safety ranger, at your service!"

Vi sat up in bed and pulled open her laptop, so she'd at least look like she was doing homework.

"You tested my alarm yesterday," Vi said gently. Blue didn't get much *gentle* from people, considering her tendency to knock doors open and shout everything she said, so Vi always tried to give her some. She'd need it, Vi figured, the older she got.

"And now it's today," Blue reasoned.

Their mother stepped into the room and rested a hand on Blue's green head. "Let's leave Violet alone right now. She's doing homework."

Her mother was beautifully dressed, as always. Perfect lipstick, crisp clothes, blond hair pulled back without any flyaways, unlike Vi's. When Vi looked at her mom, she felt something building in her chest. It had been building for days, since she found the account.

"You can take out the alarm batteries," her mom whispered, as Blue ran back down the stairs. "I promise I won't tell."

"Thanks." Vi forced a smile, and her mom winked before shutting the bedroom door.

Silence reigned again, and though Vi usually liked the quiet, today it made her itchy. She reached for her phone again, her finger hovering over the Instagram icon, but a chat notification pinged instead.

She stared at it for a few seconds, trying to comprehend. *Lucas Hill.*

Her heart stuttered.

Lucas: the second most crushed-on boy in the grade, but her personal favorite, because he was half-Asian, half-white, like her, and his hair was cute in a sleepy way, and Gregory, the most crushed-on boy, was terrible.

She was afraid to open the message. She had to open the message. The icon by his name was a miniature image of a cartoon character, color-blocked in pink and gray, and Vi thought of the prophecy. *Pink and gray both on one day.*

She couldn't help but hear Nomi. *Annihilation.*

But that was silly.

She opened the message.

ALL TREES ARE HISTORIANS, BUT SOME TREES WANT to be poets.

There's a dreamy quality to trees like these. They grow at a slant, knotted with branches bent at such strange angles that birds can't help but build nests in their nooks, and even humans can't help but notice.

We trees, we forest chorus, have learned to recognize this particular kind of botanical. They see the world in possibility, like everything's connected, like all of it matters, like anything could be a seed: the first day in spring, a phrase placed just right, an idea, a child.

And when a tree that dreams in poetry eventually becomes a book, when that book eventually finds a girl who dreams in poetry too—not even the forest knows what words they'll discover.

VI

sup

Three letters. No punctuation. Not **what's the homework?** Not **ur mom is hot.** (Vi had gotten that once from Gregory, and when she'd told Nomi, her friend had gotten so mad she'd turned red and threatened violence. Nomi wouldn't have *actually* done anything, of course. She never got in trouble.)

But there it was . . . **sup**. As if *Lucas Hill* simply wanted to talk to her.

Maybe it was a prank. Maybe he'd meant to message someone else. Vi wasn't someone boys noticed.

But she let herself believe for a second that this was real.

just homework, she wrote. It wasn't a cool answer, but it opened the door, in case he wanted to ask her a school question.

His response came quickly.

cool. what hmwrk?

She sat up fully, buzzy with adrenaline. Distantly, she was aware that this was the least eventful conversation of all time, and being so excited about it was embarrassing. But that didn't stop her hands from shaking, as if the air had suddenly grown cold.

The only homework she had left was math, and they weren't even in the same class. He was super smart, in honors math with Nomi, though he'd probably help Vi if she needed it, because he was nice, and boys liked helping girls with this kind of thing, right?

But talking about math seemed so boring, so she typed: **i'm trying to find out who wrote an old journal that nomi found.**

Three typing dots appeared and then: **oh, for that project?**

She blinked before understanding his question. Right. They had a semester-long social studies project where they were supposed to research an artifact. Nobody was working on it yet, because it wasn't due until December, and she realized belatedly that this might make her look like a teacher's pet.

But it was better than explaining the actual story: *No, we found this old book when we were kids and Nomi thinks it predicts the future. I might think so too. I mean, you'd be surprised at some of the things it got right. But now she wants to find a sequel, and I'm not sure it exists, but I don't know how to tell her no and—*

yea, she typed instead. **for social studies.**

> Nice. I like girls that care abt school.

Vi's face went hot. Was this flirting? Her thumbs hovered over the keyboard. She had no idea how to flirt back.

gotta go, he wrote.

And that was it. Her one chance at talking to Lucas Hill and she couldn't even muster a response.

But then another message came.

> **lets talk more later tho.**

And another.

> **your cool** ☺

A smiley face. A smiley face from Lucas Hill, even though boys didn't usually send smiley faces, which made this even sweeter.

Vi hugged her phone. This secret—it wasn't bitter at all. This was pure orange pulp. An unexpected burst of citrus.

She closed her eyes to savor it.

Eventually she'd have to tell her best friend.

But for a moment, she wanted to keep this for herself.

NOMI

"VIOLET'S NOT HERSELF ANYMORE," NOMI ANNOUNCED from her seat on the kitchen counter, watching as her mom slid an unfrozen frozen pizza out of the oven.

Her mom paused. "And by that you mean . . . ?"

A bead of sweat rolled down Nomi's back. Using the oven always made their cramped one-bedroom apartment approximately a million degrees too hot, but today was worse than usual. They couldn't open the windows this evening, on account of all the smoke outside, and Nomi could barely breathe. "She wants to go by Vi. And she was wearing, like, whole new clothes. Pink clothes."

"There's nothing wrong with pink." Her mom plopped the spinach pizza on the cutting board, blowing as if that would actually cool it down. "We've been trained as a society to dislike the color because—"

"Because it's associated with girls and the patriarchy looks down on girls, yeah, yeah, I know," Nomi interrupted. Whenever Nomi and her mom watched reality TV, her mom spent the commercial breaks teaching Nomi about feminism. To balance it out, et cetera.

"And there's nothing wrong with wanting a nickname, or a new name entirely," her mom added. "In fact, it's good to let people choose their identities."

"Okay, but this isn't about gender identity or anything," Nomi insisted, watching as her mom sliced the pizza. "I asked at lunch."

Her mom gave her a *look*, which was annoying, because her mom wasn't getting it. Nomi had begged Violet for an adequate explanation, and she'd gotten nothing.

"What I *mean*," Nomi clarified, "is that it's one thing if your friend wants to be *more* of themselves. That's great. But Violet wants to be *less*. She wants to be how *other* people want her to be. And aren't I obligated to do something about that? As a friend? To show her how great she is?"

Her mom loaded a steaming slice onto a plate and set it in front of Nomi. "Is it possible that maybe, just maybe, you're making this bigger than it is?"

Nomi hesitated. "Maybe." But maybe *not*. If Violet was changing her name, there had to be a reason. And maybe Nomi had a tendency to make things big, but that was because the world *was* big.

And this . . . this was Violet, shrinking. *Vi.* As if she was saying, *Don't bother with that second syllable. Don't waste your breath.*

Nomi hated that. She would've gladly spent a million

syllables on Violet. In fact, she loved her whole name: Violet Noelle Sun Ja Kim. Seven syllables! And all of them suited her best friend perfectly, thank you very much.

Gently, her mom said, "Let Vi be who she wants to be."

Nomi bit into her pizza. *Fine.* Violet was Vi now, and that was *fine* except that Nomi was in danger of losing her, the way she'd already lost Arthur.

The cheese burned the roof of her mouth as she chewed.

"Why do you want to visit Anthony's museum tomorrow?" her mom asked, changing the subject.

"I . . ." Nomi faltered. She didn't usually lie to her mom. Not out of some kind of moral principle, but because why would she? Her mom was her second-best best friend.

But her mom was also a practical person who didn't believe in prophecies, et cetera, and if Nomi mentioned that pink clothes had in fact kick-started doom, her mom would start talking about *coping strategies.*

"It's for a school project." Violet—*Vi*—had texted her that morning, **i'm telling my parents this is for social studies,** so Nomi went with that.

"That's great, hon." Her mom folded a slice in half and took a bite. She didn't even bother sitting. She worked two jobs, managing the local grocery store and logging inventory for a publisher, and she was so busy that she seemed to forget sitting was an option. "It'll be nice to see Anthony. I haven't seen him in ages."

Nomi nodded. Their parents had been close, but when

Nomi and Arthur stopped talking, their parents stopped hanging out so much, which seemed sad and almost scary to Nomi.

Friendships, she'd decided, were almost as unreliable as the future. But the book would fix everything. It would make the world right again.

ARTHUR

WHEN ARTHUR RAN, THE WORLD BELONGED TO HIM.

It didn't used to be that way. He'd been kinda slow and small—and then *bam*. He'd grown five inches last year and suddenly he could hold his own. Better than that, actually. He was good, especially in cross-country, all speed and strength.

And the first meet of the season couldn't have come at a better time. He'd spent the previous night worrying the schools would cancel it due to smoke, and though some parents were mad when they didn't, Arthur was thrilled—he'd keep running even if the world was on fire.

When he ran, he didn't need to think about things like Nomi and her obsession with that old diary. He didn't need to think about how much time they'd spent looking over those pages together, decoding lines like they were searching for treasure. He didn't need to think about the way she sat up straighter when she had an idea, or the way her knees bounced when she got excited, or the way her hair swished like it had its own gravity.

All he needed to think about was the dirt beneath his feet and the West Seattle pines above his head.

"Artsy, my guy!" Lucas ran up alongside him and clapped him on the shoulder. Arthur pretended it didn't knock some of the wind out of him.

If Arthur was a good runner, Lucas was great, by far the best on the team, and Arthur felt a weird slush of envy and pride, because Lucas had chosen him as a friend. It was a new friendship, just a year old, and Arthur wasn't about to mess it up, not when Lucas had saved him from total isolation last year. Not when being friends with Lucas meant being friends with the whole cross country group.

"Hey." Normally, Arthur didn't like talking during meets, but this was the first one, more of a practice than anything else, and they were way better than the other school.

"Saw you talking to Know-It-All Nomi yesterday," Lucas said, with a laugh in his voice. "She really trapped you. Condolences, man."

Arthur didn't know what *condolences* meant, and he wasn't about to ask. "Oh yeah. She wanted to talk about . . . a social studies question," he lied. It was the only class he and Nomi had together, because every other class she took was honors level.

Lucas and Arthur never talked about Arthur's Nomi-Violet years. It wasn't a big deal, of course, but neither of them ever mentioned it, which made it seem like it was at least *a* deal.

Lucas grinned at him with perfectly straight teeth. He hadn't needed braces. "You're with Violet, then!"

Arthur felt like he'd missed a step in this conversation. "What?"

"Violet told me she's in Nomi's group for the social studies project. Looking for a journal or something."

"Oh." Arthur had no idea what to make of the fact that, apparently, Vi and Lucas talked. It felt too weird to ask about. And it seemed that Arthur and Vi had both stumbled into the same lie, which made the lie bigger. Like, no longer a white lie. A gray lie. "Um, I'm thinking about changing groups, though."

Fixed it.

"Ah, man, come on." Lucas rolled his eyes like Arthur had done something wrong. Somehow, whenever Nomi and Vi got involved, Arthur had the feeling of doing something wrong. "You gotta stay. Get me that inside info."

"About our social studies project?"

Lucas laughed. "About Violet."

"Oh, um . . ." Was this some weird way of making fun of Arthur for being friends with them years ago? He tried to tread lightly. "She actually goes by Vi now, I think. I'm not really sure why or . . ."

"See! That's the inside info I'm talking about. Vi." Lucas tasted the name. Behind them, a handful of their other teammates were catching up, and when Lucas picked up the pace, Arthur attempted to match it. "That's even hotter."

Arthur was getting winded. Maybe the smoke was getting to him. "Uh . . ." he said.

"Uhhh . . ." Lucas mimicked, though not in a mean way. Mostly. "Look, I've gotta ask."

A ball of dread knotted in Arthur's stomach. Or maybe it was just side pain. He needed to slow down.

"I know there's something you're not telling," Lucas continued. "You're a bad liar."

The ball grew larger, and Arthur stumbled over a root before righting himself. His footsteps pounded *Nomi, Nomi, Nomi.*

Lucas lowered his voice, "Are you gay?"

The dread evaporated. Arthur tried not to look relieved. "What? No."

Lucas grinned. "Dude, you don't have to be embarrassed."

Arthur considered lying, just to get out of this conversation. But he was a bad liar. "I'm not gay."

"Oh, come on. I'm not, like, eighty years old. I don't care about that stuff." Lucas waggled his brows. "As long as you like someone good. It's me, isn't it?"

Arthur snorted. "You wish."

Lucas laughed, and Arthur felt like he could breathe again. Running was easy. Lucas didn't suspect anything social-life-imploding about him and Nomi. Compared to that, Lucas thinking he was gay was whatever.

"Look," Lucas said, "I'm all in favor of your newfound sexual awakening. Less competition for me. But you gotta do me a favor."

"Yeah?" Arthur's voice was as light as he felt.

"Stay in that social studies group. Get back in Vi's good graces and put in a good word for me, you know?"

Lucas said this like it was nothing, but spending time with Vi meant spending time with Nomi. And there was something about Nomi that would eat Arthur alive, if he let it.

He opened his mouth to say no way, not a chance, terrible idea. But then Lucas added, "Please? You're the only guy I trust."

It felt pretty nice, to be trusted, and when Arthur opened his mouth, what came out was "Sure."

Lucas grinned. "I knew I could count on you, Artsy." He slapped Arthur's back again, and then he ran faster, leaving Arthur behind.

Arthur tried to manage his heart rate. He'd interact with the girls a little, enough to put in a good word for Lucas, whatever that meant. And that would be it. He'd keep his distance. Nothing bad could possibly happen.

WE TREES KNOW WHEN SOMETHING BAD IS GOING TO happen.

You might call it a sixth sense, but we don't measure our senses that way, don't plant fences between sensing and feeling and knowing.

What we sense, feel, know: Lifetimes ago, there was a girl—a seed—scattered to the wind to root in a place not yet called Seattle. She felt lost on this land—where others had rooted first, and us before that, where her father had brought her and she did not choose to be—until her father handed her a notebook (a tree, a poet, though she didn't know it).

What do I write? she asked.

Most of the time, humans don't hear us. It's okay. We're used to it. But every once in a while one does, and we answered her, our words whispering through leaves, like a rustling, like a song:

Find your forest. Deepen roots. Build a canopy.

So she began to talk to people. She asked everyone she

met what they had to say, foraging for wisdom, building a common language out of English and the Mandarin and Lushootseed words she'd started to gather.

When the kids on Front Street taught her a new game, she wrote—*Count to twenty before you jump.*

When the fisherwoman sold her the morning catch—*Never take more than you need.*

When the men in the lumberyard warned her which trees were too brittle to climb in autumn—*When leaves flutter, too high to climb, too far to fall.*

The girl wrote all of it down.

Those: seeds, too. A chorus of ideas, a forest, growing by the day, until the girl, looking for more, entered a shop on the corner of First and Madison and set the future in motion.

Be careful, we told her. *Something is about to happen.*

It had been a sunny spring, without enough rain.

NOMI

THE FIRST THING THAT HIT NOMI WHEN SHE STEPPED into the Museum of Lost and Found on the corner of First and Madison was the scent: crinkled paper, lemon, and a hint of firewood, the way her memory smelled.

The living room–turned-gallery was crowded with art and color, each wall a feast of paintings, photographs, and little pencil sketches. The center of the room was a labyrinth of sculptures, and the far corner was stuffed with bookshelves and manuscripts.

The layout was the same as Nomi remembered, but all the art was different—and the strange collision of familiar and new made her brain itch. It was like remembering the lyrics to a song she'd forgotten—only to realize the melody had changed.

"Carrie! It's been forever!" Arthur's dad Anthony stepped out from behind a desk in the corner and squeezed Nomi's mom before turning his attention to the girls. "Arthur told me you two would stop by. For your social studies project?"

Nomi glanced at Vi. She must have told Arthur to use the same lie, which meant they'd *talked*? Without her? The thought felt prickly-weird.

But Vi seemed just as surprised by the comment. "Oh, um . . ." She recovered quickly. "Yeah! We're supposed to find an artifact to study. And we knew just where to find one."

Nomi could tell Vi was lying, of course, considering the best-friend superpower. And also considering that this was *not* their social studies project.

But if they *hadn't* been best friends forever . . . well, it was impressive and a little bit scary how smoothly Vi lied.

"Vi's telling the truth," Nomi added, which only made it sound less true, but neither parent noticed.

Anthony's eyes crinkled when he smiled at her, and Nomi realized she'd missed him. He had a way of making her feel instantly welcome. "Pick anything," he said, gesturing to the gallery.

The girls thanked him and Nomi tugged Vi away from the parents, toward the maze of manuscripts. The shelves were smaller than she remembered, or maybe she'd just grown. No matter. She ran her fingertips along the old spines and binder clips until she found it.

The book of prophecies.

She hadn't held it in so long, but it still felt magical—brown leather cover, heavy paper, looping lines of text. She thumbed her way through the water-warped pages, which rustled as if to say hello. Nomi shivered.

"Remember when it told me to check my old backpack," Vi said, smiling a little, "and I found five dollars?"

In bags threadbare, coin to spare.

How could Nomi possibly forget? She'd filed away every prediction in her head. "Or when it predicted Mr. Anderson would change the seating assignment," she said, "and I had to sit by Samuel?"

Rearranging furniture can lead to discomfort.

Samuel was a nice kid now, but back in fifth grade, he used to pick his nose and wipe his boogers under the desk, right between him and Nomi.

Vi cringed. "Seating arrangements are cruel and unnecessary."

"Totally!" Nomi agreed. "And that wasn't even as bad as when I had to sit by horrible Gregory and Lucas last year."

Vi's smile faltered for a millisecond before she said, "What about when the book knew Arthur would get food poisoning from those week-old tacos?"

"To be fair, we knew that too."

Vi snorted, and when they locked eyes, Nomi felt yesterday's weirdness fade. They were Nomi and Violet again, best friends forever. Or, well, Nomi and Vi, at least.

Nomi flipped to the final page and read, "'How do you

turn a girl to flame? When canopies burn, you'll never be the same.'" She let her voice trail off before looking up.

"Yeah . . ." Vi acknowledged. "That one's intense."

"Super ominous," Nomi said ominously.

"'When canopies burn . . .'" Vi murmured. "Is that referring to the current wildfires?"

"It must be," Nomi said. "The forest canopies are burning. Which means we don't have much time to find the sequel."

Vi hesitated, like she didn't want to ask her question. "And how exactly are we gonna find it?"

From behind them, the floorboards creaked, and a voice said, "I could, uh, help you?"

Nomi spun around to find Arthur standing behind a shelf. Her stomach folded in half. "Arthur?"

He shrugged, almost apologetically, as if to say, *Yes sorry, it is in fact me.*

Heat flared in her. The *nerve* of him to look sorry, when he'd never said sorry for anything at all.

When he'd started avoiding her, when she'd realized the friendship-ending prophecy was about *him*, she'd tried to prevent it. She'd told him: *I think this is about us,* and he'd responded: *Chill, Nomi. It's just a book.*

A friendship ends with a crush. Too much.

It *was* crushing. It crushed her to know that all those years of friendship meant nothing to him. She meant nothing to him.

Because he hadn't talked to her after that. He'd stopped inviting her and Vi over, and he avoided them at school. It was like Lucas came along, and suddenly Arthur was too cool for them. He hadn't needed them anymore. So then, *fine*.

She was about to tell him they didn't need him either, not at all—but for once, Vi beat her to words.

"How could you help?" Vi asked. The words sounded far kinder in her mouth than they would've in Nomi's.

Arthur looked pained, as if talking to them actually hurt. Well. "I don't know . . . Research? Um . . . Google?"

"We've obviously *googled*," Nomi said.

Vi shot her a look, which probably meant *Be nice*, but which Nomi decided to interpret as *Be nice to him, with your saintly powers of patience, though he is so far beneath us, and does not deserve such generosity.*

Nomi nodded to say, *Thanks, friend.*

Arthur looked back and forth between them and frowned. "I mean, did you search the final prophecy?"

Nomi blinked. "Uh . . ."

Arthur turned red. "Never mind."

Nomi had searched the statistical possibility of prophecies (variable answers from different religious websites), and how predictions worked (lots of information on weather tracking), and even searched for stories about old books (an infinite number of listicles about classic literature), but she hadn't searched the prophecies themselves. She didn't know why, exactly, except that they felt so separate from the internet. Typing them into a search bar felt . . . silly. Childish.

But maybe Arthur had a point.

"You have a point," she admitted.

"I do?" Arthur opened and closed his mouth, as if words completely failed him. "Uh, okay. Then, um. Follow me."

He led them past Anthony and Nomi's mom—who were having a much happier reunion than Arthur and Nomi—and took them up the stairs, out of the museum, and into his apartment.

Nomi had spent tons of time there. She and her mom, and sometimes Vi and her parents, had spent nearly every Friday evening there for years. They'd light candles and eat dinner, and hanging out had felt easy in a way Nomi could barely remember.

Back then, she could've walked through the kitchen, gotten herself a glass of grape juice, and peeled herself a clementine without asking permission. Now she felt like a stranger.

"Wait here," Arthur said before disappearing into his bedroom.

Vi leaned over. "It's weird being here, right?"

"So weird!" Nomi exclaimed, before remembering to whisper. She dropped her voice. *"Completely bizarre."*

After all this time, it was like seeing the apartment with new eyes. It wasn't quite as nice as Vi's house, but it was four blocks from the Seattle Public Library and three blocks from Pike Place Market, which was pretty cool, and it had three bedrooms—Arthur's, his dads', and an office.

Envy twisted behind Nomi's ribs. Her mom had given

her the only bedroom in their apartment, which meant her mom slept on a foldout couch. Most times, not having a dad didn't really affect Nomi, but having enough money seemed basically impossible without two parents, and even though Nomi's mom tried to shield her from money stuff, Nomi couldn't help but feel the crushing weight of *almost not enough.*

Arthur emerged from his room and set his open laptop on the dining table. "I don't know what to search," he said.

Nomi hesitated before sitting in front of his computer. She felt even more like an intruder as her fingers hovered over his keyboard. But she knew what to type. The phrases were a piece of her, imprinted on her memory.

She searched a few of the prophecies at random, typing words that felt too monumental for Google. The first few searches yielded very little: message-board posts and random businesses and some YouTube videos—pranks, shopping hauls, an old *SNL* skit.

"Okay, this was a stupid idea," Arthur said, reaching to take his laptop back.

But Nomi stopped him. "Just let me try . . ."

She typed the final prophecy.

Pink and gray both on one day.

And then on and on, each line feeling bigger, until her fingers were vibrating.

She hit enter.

The top hit was a video, a TED Talk entitled "What the Trees Have to Say," which Nomi was ready to ignore, but Vi reached over to click it. A woman with deep brown skin, thin braids, and blue glasses appeared on the screen, smiling softly as the applause faded around her.

"Thank you all for coming," she said, her voice distorted through Arthur's speakers. "Today, I'd like to talk about trees."

"This doesn't have anything to do with the book," Arthur interrupted.

But Nomi sped through the video, skimming the captions until—

"It reminds me of something I read once," the woman said, about halfway through her speech. Nomi slowed the video to normal speed as the woman grew serious. And maybe Nomi was being dramatic, but she *knew* the look on the woman's face—that mixture of awe and fear, like the words she was about to say were special. "When the world turns rough, we know too much and not enough." She trailed off, seemingly lost in thought.

Nomi stopped the video, heart pounding. The woman had changed a few words, but that was it: a line from the prophecy.

"That's not the exact quote though, right?" Vi asked. "It could be a coincidence?"

"No," Arthur murmured. "I mean, it doesn't seem like a coincidence."

Nomi turned to him, surprised by the intensity in his

voice—but when he saw her looking he flushed red again, like he was embarrassed to care.

She shook her head. There were more important things to focus on.

"Me neither," she said. She pulled the speaker's name from the video description and searched it in Google.

Dr. Clarice Newman.

"She's a professor." A link to the University of Washington faculty page popped up, and Nomi clicked through it. "She studies trees."

Nomi's heart pounded. They'd found her: the author of the book—*books*.

The final prophecy had started, and the future was hurtling toward them, nearly in reach.

Nomi leaned forward, one thousand percent determined. "And we're going to meet her."

PART II

✦

*Tell me now, when the world turned rough–
Two know too much, one not enough.*

VI

VI PUSHED HER ZUCCHINI NOODLES ACROSS HER dinner plate, but it was hard to feel hungry.

Yesterday, Nomi had done her Level 5 Nomi thing and scheduled a meeting with the professor as soon as possible, which meant they were planning to see her after school tomorrow. Nomi, of course, had found it excruciating to wait through the weekend. But Vi hadn't minded. The promise of annihilation, as Nomi would not stop calling it, pounded inside Vi's skull, and she just wanted to forget.

Thankfully, she had a pretty good distraction.

She and Lucas had chatted basically nonstop since she got home from the museum yesterday, and they'd stayed up so late that she'd slept until noon.

Middle schoolers, Blue had muttered, with an exaggerated eye roll.

In their chats, Vi and Lucas talked about nothing and everything, their conversation floating as freely as smoke. They talked about their Girl Scout cookie ranking (Thin Mints, Samoas, Tagalongs), about homework overload, about how parents just didn't get it—and sometimes friends didn't either.

Now, throughout dinner, Lucas was texting her about Gregory, and she positioned her phone under the table to read it.

gregory wont stop talking about how much his gf trusts him, he wrote.

that's kinda annoying, she typed back.

He responded with a string of texts:

> **srsly. idk i think people trust me too but maybe not.**

> **i kinda worry about that.**

> **sry i shouldnt dump all this on a pretty girl.**

An unfamiliar kind of pleasure hiccupped inside her. It wasn't just the *pretty girl* compliment—though she cupped that to her heart like a newborn butterfly.

It was the trust. It was the fact that he could tell her how he felt—*Lucas* of all people, Lucas, who was cool enough to float above feelings. It was the most obvious of surprises to find out that he had feelings too. It was the most shocking of surprises to learn that he trusted her with them.

His secrets were tangy and unexpectedly sweet, like the ripened blackberries lining Seattle's sidewalks.

Lol don't worry about it, she wrote—before deleting it. Too casual.

She typed, **I mean, don't worry about telling me.** Deleted. Too serious.

Finally, she sent, **I'm sure tons of people trust you.**

"Vi, I need you to put the phone away while we're at the table," her mom said.

Vi could have pointed out that her mom spent the entire day on her phone. In the pickup line at school? On the phone. In the grocery store? On the phone. When Vi was talking about her day? On the phone, periodically, but only when Vi had been going on too long.

But Vi did not point that out. She slid her phone into her pocket and took a bite of zoodles. Zucchini should just be zucchini, she decided. It wasn't fooling anyone by pretending to be noodles.

Her dad went back to talking about work, about in-person office policies and promotion tracks and Vanessa the assistant who kept mixing up meetings but was nice and needed the money and should he put Vanessa on a promotion track, maybe? It was the most boring conversation Vi could imagine.

Across the table, Blue made a face at Vi, like she thought so, too.

"Amazon could really help Vanessa," their dad continued, "if she let us. I gave her a big advertising opportunity last year, but she never really rose to the challenge."

Their dad was busy with work most of the time, and

when he wasn't, he was talking about it. Which was fine, except sometimes he felt like a stranger to Vi.

"Amazon is on fire," Blue interjected, because she'd gone a valiant forty minutes without talking about fire safety.

"No, honey, the wildfire is far away, in the mountains," their mom reassured her. "Amazon is perfectly safe."

"She means the rainforest," Vi clarified.

"Oh," their mom said. "Well, yes."

Their dad's fork scraped against the plate as it twirled. "Blue, we're going to be fine. The Amazon rainforest is on an entirely different continent." Turning to their mom, he added, "I don't know why this school insists on teaching second graders these things."

He looked pointedly at the pile of batteries on the kitchen counter. Blue's safety testing had gotten so insistent and disruptive that their parents had gathered the smoke alarms and excavated the batteries, like surgeons extracting a heart.

"We can save the world," Blue declared.

Their mom looked, briefly, like she was going to cry. In moments like these (which were becoming increasingly common), Vi felt like she herself might float away, like her soul might leave her body, like she might not have a body at all.

She pinched her leg, zapping herself back to reality. "I'm meeting a tree teacher tomorrow," she said, and then, feeling silly, clarified, "I mean a botany professor."

"You are?" her mom asked.

"Arthur's dad is taking us," she explained, realizing too

late that she'd never asked her own parents' permission. "If that's okay."

"For that artifact project?"

Vi looked down at her dinner. She could feel her mom's eyes on her. "Yeah."

Her dad spoke up. "That sounds like a sensible school project. Better than thinking about how the world's on fire."

"The polar bears are dying," Blue informed them.

"Oh Christ," their dad replied.

In Vi's pocket, her phone buzzed, and her whole body burned to check. How upset would her mom be? She slid her fingers toward her pocket and tilted the screen up.

Nah, gregory's gf sends him pics and idk, Lucas typed. **Nobody's ever trusted me that much.**

"Anyway!" her mom exclaimed, so loudly everyone jumped. Vi shoved the phone back into her pocket. "Vi, are you excited for your first ever middle school dance?"

Vi tried not to think too hard about Lucas's text. She hadn't paid much attention to the upcoming dance, but the more she texted Lucas, the more the event lingered in the back of her mind, growing more and more present.

Every year, a handful of seventh- and eighth-grade volunteers worked with some teachers to put on a big fundraising dance—FunDance, though nobody actually called it that. This year, funds were going to the Forest Service. Trees, trees, and more trees—Vi hadn't thought this much about trees since her childhood obsession with *The Giving Tree,* a book that had, for reasons she couldn't understand, made her want to cry.

"It's not really a dance," Vi said carefully. "It's just like . . . seventh graders pretending it's a dance."

She'd heard an eighth grader say that in the hallway, and it seemed right. At least right enough. Never mind that thinking of it now made her heart hitch somewhere between panic and excitement.

Her mom frowned. "Of course it's real. We should get you a dress. Do you want a dress?"

"Vi has six thousand dresses," Blue interjected.

"I have four," Vi said.

Their mom nodded sagely. "Four isn't nearly enough. Let's go shopping."

Vi's phone buzzed again with Lucas's words. She checked the message, her pulse beating in her fingertips.

> sry, forget i said anything.
> wanna play a game?

"Oh boy," their dad said. His eyes twinkled at his wife, like he found her endlessly amusing. "Girl stuff."

He wasn't being mean, but something in his tone made Vi feel restless, and she couldn't look at him. Her phone burned in her pocket, and maybe she really would need a dress for the dance. "Yeah," she said, turning back to her mom. "I'd like that."

ARTHUR

ARTHUR WASN'T EVEN THINKING ABOUT THE DANCE.

Like, at all, pretty much. He didn't care about things like dances, or girls like Nomi, or magical books that told the future.

Arthur was focused, entirely and completely, on helping his dad unpack a box of lumpy pottery. Someone had left it on the doorstep, and Arthur had found the tilting vases that evening, packed into a cardboard box that was just about ready to give up.

Arthur didn't get why people left their art at the museum. If they thought it was good, why wouldn't they put their name on it? And if they *didn't* think it was good, why on earth would they want anyone else to see it?

"Arthur."

Arthur looked up to see Danthony's raised brow. He knew this expression. His dad had been trying to get his attention for some time now.

"Sorry," Arthur mumbled. "What?"

"Will you get the display stands so we can put these vases out on the floor?"

Arthur tried not to look too relieved as he left his dad by the computer. Logging new inventory was the worst, and his dad's spreadsheet system made Arthur's head go numb. He never knew what parts of an art piece he was supposed to focus on. Type of art, sure. Quantity, obvious. But then there was the other stuff, the art part his dad just seemed to get.

Three vases, Danthony wrote. *Clayware. Speckled with blue glaze. A hint of playfulness, like the color is intentionally accidental. Fresh, too, like the sculptor pulled it straight from the ground. FTE?*

His dad wrote abbreviations into his notes all the time, which Arthur had stopped trying to decode.

He pulled a stand out of the storage closet.

The thing was, Nomi kept treating him like he'd done something wrong. Which was unfair. FTE. Frankly, Too Extreme.

Friendships drifted all the time. It wasn't like he'd done anything bad.

He carried the stand into the center of the room, the heavy tug at his muscles feeling like relief.

Yesterday, when he'd stepped into the museum and seen her, he'd felt the familiar pounding, like his body would never return to normal functioning.

And then, the whole rest of the day, his eyes jumped toward her, hoping she wouldn't notice. He hated that sick feeling of 20 percent wanting to see her and 80 percent wanting the exact opposite. More than anything, he hated that he *still* felt that way.

He brought the vases over and arranged them on the stand.

After a year without talking to her, he should have been cured. And if that wasn't enough, seeing her through Lucas's eyes should've done it: Know-It-All Nomi, of the wild hair and the FTE habit of shoving her intelligence in everyone's faces.

But—his traitorous mind supplied—it was kinda cool how smart she was. How excited she got when she learned something new.

Whatever. Now the whole tree-professor thing was making him think of that first year of friendship. They'd been in the same first-grade class, and Danthony, Nomi's mom, and Vi's mom had all met at an open house. The parents hit it off instantly, which meant the kids started carpooling.

They'd wait together at the pickup after school, under the big oak tree, and Nomi would tell stories about all the people in all of history (thousands of years, she'd claimed, which Arthur had believed) who'd sat under that tree.

There are magical messages carved into this tree, Nomi had insisted. *I can feel it.*

The stories were always over the top and FTE, because she was a first grader, and she was Nomi, and though the kids never actually found any bark-carved messages, Vi and Arthur had been captivated.

In the years after, Nomi stopped making up stories. She'd go on and on about how she didn't believe in magic. But despite that, she'd managed to convince him that a freaking *tree* was magical. And then she'd done the same thing for a book. It was just how she was—she herself was kinda magic, and she didn't even know it.

He stepped back and squinted at the vases. They looked wrong, like there was a perfect arrangement and he couldn't quite find it.

It was going to be so awkward with Nomi tomorrow.

He sighed. At least he wasn't thinking about the dance.

VI

THE TENSION BETWEEN ARTHUR AND NOMI WAS THICK as smoke, and Vi had the unfortunate task of sitting between them. They were in the back of Anthony's car, driving to the university to meet the professor.

Vi was surprised by her own nerves. She'd told herself she didn't care much about the book, that it was Nomi's thing—but now, as they grew closer, she couldn't deny the swoop in her stomach. The book had been a mystery for so long, and finally, they were about to get answers.

Except . . . sometimes, Vi wasn't sure she wanted the answers. She didn't want a book to know her future better than she did. What if she wanted to surprise people? What if she wanted to surprise herself? There was something exciting about *not* knowing, about climbing into the future and discovering what it had in store for her.

Arthur shifted by her side. Then Nomi. Both of them were staring out their windows in an intense way that silently said, rather loudly, that they were *not* looking at each other.

Like Nomi, Vi was hurt by the way Arthur had ended their friendship. He'd stopped talking to them almost overnight, which had left the friendship hanging, unfinished. She didn't know why he'd cut them off, but she'd never been as close with him as Nomi had, so it didn't bother her as much. If anything, having Nomi to herself had been kind of nice.

Arthur looked at Nomi, then turned away.

Nomi looked at Arthur, then turned away.

Vi sighed and looked out Arthur's window.

The smoke was worse today. It blurred the skyline to a smear of gray, making Seattle feel small with an edge of unreality. If she hadn't known better, she might have believed that beyond the gray was just . . . nothing, as if the city were a painting in Anthony's museum, abandoned by the artist when it got too hard.

It made her feel like if she walked too far, she too might cease to exist.

"They changed the sign," Nomi said, slicing through the silence.

"What sign?" Arthur asked.

Vi knew without even looking. They were driving past the digital billboard, the one that simultaneously annoyed and fascinated Nomi. It changed every few days, and whenever it did, she would text Vi an update.

It says "open your eyes."

Today it says "turn mud into love."

Now it's "the wheel keeps turning." WHAT could that possibly mean? WHY is that on a billboard?

"I guess whoever changes the sign realized 'Breathe' was a weird thing to say during the smoke," Nomi said.

"'Seeing is a flower.'" Anthony read the new text aloud. "Huh. Not sure what that means."

It didn't mean anything of course. And yet, Vi's heart hitched as her eyes landed on the billboard, simple black text over white.

Seeing is a flower.

Maybe it was the smoke, rendering this big impersonal city into a small personal bubble, because ridiculously, Vi felt like the sign was personally taunting her. Everyone, even this strange billboard, saw her as her mother's little flower. Everyone except . . .

The game Lucas proposed last night had turned out to be a game of secrets, of trading hidden pieces of themselves.

Each text from him had given Vi so much energy that she'd had to walk circles around her room before sitting down to reply, and she'd discovered, circling the pitch-dark privacy of her bedroom, that he was scared of spiders, that he'd learned to read later than all his friends, and that sometimes he wondered if he even liked cross-country.

Vi confessed that she, too, hated spiders, that she actually liked school, and that the question *What do you want to be when you grow up?* sent her into a full panic. And though she didn't share her biggest secret, didn't tell him the way

Raising Wildflowers sat behind her brows like a headache, by the time she went to sleep, she felt like she actually knew him.

And somehow, he knew her. He saw her.

Vi had known Nomi since they were six, which meant Nomi knew Vi better than anyone else. But it also meant there was a version of Vi that was Nomi's: a collection of things Nomi liked about her—the way her jokes made Nomi laugh, the way her comments made Nomi think, memories and mis-memories and everything, all of it, for six years.

But with Lucas, Vi was new.

Something swelled in her chest, something bigger than a crush. Not love—she wasn't that silly. Not even puppy love, or anything near it. But . . . something.

Arthur's dad pulled into the university parking lot, and all four of them filed out of the car.

"Masks on," Anthony reminded them, and Vi slid hers on to shield from the smoke—a flowered fabric mask sewn by her grandmother during Covid. Back then, people thought that the world might be ending, but now here was Vi, in a world painted gray, unfinished, without any end at all.

Nomi rushed ahead without bothering to wait, so Vi slowed enough to walk beside Arthur. "Hey," she said.

He looked a little startled. "Hi."

"I . . ." she forced herself to ask, before she could regret it. "You're friends with Lucas, right?" Of course he was. She knew that.

"Oh." He looked surprised, then guilty. "Right. He actually asked me to—Yeah."

She wasn't sure why he was acting strange—guilt over ending the friendship with her and Nomi, possibly. But she wasn't looking for an apology.

For now . . . she wasn't sure why this felt so important, but Nomi hated Lucas, which made it hard not to question . . .

"Do you trust him?" she blurted. Lucas hadn't mentioned the photos from Gregory's girlfriend again, and Vi hadn't asked, though she'd wanted to. She didn't know for sure what he was talking about, but she had a guess.

Arthur adjusted his mask, like it didn't fit right on his face. "Of course. He's cool. He's my guy."

"Right." Vi let herself relax. She was texting with a boy Arthur trusted, a boy who knew her and saw her, and she could be anything. "Thanks."

"Almost there!" Nomi called back to them, voice giddy. "Second book, here we come. That prophecy is no match for us."

Vi grinned at Nomi and quickened her pace, but as the science building loomed up ahead, the final prophetic line rang in her ears. *You'll never be the same.*

Maybe that wasn't such a bad thing.

NOMI

FINDING THE BOOK OF PROPHECIES WAS THE BEST thing that ever happened to Nomi. And finding the second book would be the second best.

See, everything in life could be separated into two categories: fact and feeling.

For everyone else in the world, the future fell into the unreliable feelings category. You could have a *feeling* about the future, but what did that even mean?

Years ago, Nomi had had the *feeling* that everything would be okay, but you can't plan for feelings, especially when they're wrong. Especially when your mom gets laid off, and you have to move to a tiny apartment, and you can't afford your school without a scholarship, et cetera.

But then Nomi found the book—and the book turned the future into facts she could plan for.

If her life went according to plan, which it would, she would finish up her scholarship at Pineview Academy, the best K–8 school, then get a scholarship for Lamarr STEM High, the best high school, and then she'd get a full-ride to UW for college—honors program, of course—and then she'd get a really great job, and she'd be able to buy a house for her mom, and herself, too.

She could hardly contain the zip of her energy as they walked into UW's botany wing. She breathed deeply as they navigated the halls, filling her lungs with the scent of disinfectant and science and certainty.

Anthony led the way until they were standing in front of Professor Newman's office.

"Thanks," Nomi told him as she buzzed with excitement. "We'll handle things from here."

Anthony laughed. "I've never once doubted your ability to handle things, Nomi. But I'd like to meet this person first."

Nomi tried not to be impatient, but anticipation radiated from her skull to her toes. She bounced a little. *Fine.* The adults would meet, confirm their safety, and *then* they'd get to the book.

She knocked, and the door opened to reveal Professor Newman, a decade older than she'd appeared in the video. She wore an orange headscarf, big glasses, and a tweed blazer, and though her deep brown skin and wide eyes were the same, her smile seemed kinder, the slope of her shoulders softer.

Anthony introduced himself, thanked her for her time, and explained that the kids were there for school—all while Nomi tried not to burst. Vi set her hand on Nomi's elbow, a tiny gesture that let Nomi exist a little easier in her own body.

How could she possibly deserve a friend like Vi?

Finally, Anthony deemed the professor not a child murderer, probably, and stepped outside to let them talk.

The office was meticulously organized and color-coded. Exactly Nomi's kind of office. The office of a person who would write a prophecy book that ordered the world. As soon as they were alone, Nomi's words tumbled out in a single breath, a sentence strung together. "Hi I'm Nomi and this is VioletImeanVi—that's new—andthisisArthur."

"That's right." Professor Newman's eyes sparkled as she shook Nomi's hand. "I liked your email."

"Thank you!" Nomi shot a grateful look at Vi. They'd gone back and forth a bit with email drafts.

Nomi's first draft:

Salutations, Professor Newman, we require more information about a very important book at the Museum of Lost and Found. We believe it tells the future (backed up by collected scientific evidence), and based on your Ted Talk we think you might know the location of its sequel.

After Vi's edits:

Dear Professor Newman, we are looking for more information about a very important book at the Museum of Lost and Found. We like your Ted Talk! This is for school.

Nomi pulled the old journal out of her backpack. "This is the book."

"It's from my dad's museum," Arthur added.

Professor Newman took the book, holding it carefully as she slowly turned the pages.

Nomi ached with the waiting.

"I haven't seen this in so long," the professor murmured.

"So you *were* quoting it in your speech!" Nomi bounced. "I knew it! We have so many questions. Like, how did you write all this? Did you just make it up? Or did you get, like . . . visions? I don't know. Some of it just—well, anyway. What did you mean about this last prophecy? The girl and the flame? And can we please, please see the sequel?"

Gently, the professor closed the book. "Those are all great questions. I have some of the same questions myself."

Nomi frowned. "But . . ."

"Unfortunately, I can't answer them," the professor continued. "Because I didn't write it."

"Oh." It was like someone had stolen all the air. Where were they supposed to go from there? How was Nomi supposed to *breathe*?

Nomi turned to Vi, as if her friend might know what to say, but Vi looked just as confused.

It was Arthur who finally spoke. "So, if you didn't write it, who did?"

Right, a follow-up question. Nomi felt, rather begrudgingly, grateful to him.

"I found the books when I was younger, in my great-aunt's attic."

Vi tilted her head. "Your great-aunt wrote them?"

"Books, *plural!*" Nomi exclaimed. "So you do know about the sequel!"

Cautiously, Professor Newman set the book on the desk in front of her, almost as if it scared her. "Yes, there were two books. I remember that. But, no, my great-aunt didn't write them. She liked to collect old things, little pieces of the past. I'm not sure how this one ended up at your father's museum, though. I never thought I'd see it again."

Nomi tried to remain calm. "Can we meet her?"

The professor hesitated. "She died a few months ago."

"Oh," Nomi breathed. "Sorry." And she was sorry. She was terribly sorry, and trying really hard not to be *selfishly* sorry. But: a few *months*! If they'd met the professor in the summer . . . "Do you know what she did with the second book?" Nomi asked.

The professor paused, studying them over her glasses. "You have a school project, and you could have chosen anything." Her eyes drifted to the cover before she dragged her gaze back to the kids. "Yet you chose this book. Why?"

"Because the fate of the world depends on it," Nomi blurted.

Arthur gave a little cough, and Nomi realized she'd gone too far.

"I mean, *our* fate depends on it," she corrected.

Vi chimed in. "Our *grade* depends on it."

"Right," Nomi corrected her correction. "For school."

The professor chewed her cheek, and Nomi had the horrible feeling that she'd answered wrong. "Plus," Nomi added, "there's something special about it. I really, really don't believe in magic. But . . . it's close."

She could feel Vi's and Arthur's eyes on her, but she didn't dare look. Her cheeks grew hot.

But the professor's lips lifted. "I thought the same thing when I was your age."

She opened the book, running her weathered fingers over weathered pages. "I love paper like this, where you can really see its former life. This might sound corny, or even unscientific, but I always thought part of the book's magic came from the tree itself."

It was strange seeing a scientist talk like that about magic. Nomi didn't know that was allowed.

Professor Newman looked up at them. "I'm sorry I can't tell you who wrote the words, but maybe I can still tell you something useful."

Nomi nodded, desperate. She needed *something*. "Please."

"Trees have memory. If you take a piece of a tree's trunk, all the way to its core, its rings will tell a story. Each ring is a different year, and you'll see the wet years and dry years, the hot and the hungry, the fires and drought, all the growth and pain a tree has felt. You'll find the whole past laid out there."

Nomi had always tried to picture the poet, but thinking about the pages, about the tree itself, made her uncomfortable in a way she couldn't explain. She wanted concrete answers.

Arthur made a strangled noise. "Trees feel pain?"

Nomi turned to him. She hadn't even thought about

that part. But he had. Which was weird, because it wasn't an Arthur thing to notice. At least, it didn't seem like an Arthur thing to notice.

The professor's eyes softened. "This is what I get for waxing poetic. No, no, don't worry. They don't have a nervous system or a brain, so they don't feel pain the way we do. And yet . . . we know they react to painful stimuli, releasing a kind of painkiller into their system. And we know they can communicate through their root networks, warning one another of danger."

"Okay," Arthur murmured.

"It's thrilling what scientists know," she said. "Almost as thrilling as what we don't *yet* know."

Arthur didn't look thrilled. He looked ill. Nomi wondered if she should say something, just to make him feel better, but that didn't make sense, because she had no interest in making Arthur feel better. Besides, she was too busy feeling ill herself.

There was so much they *did not yet know* about the book, and that wasn't thrilling at all!

"I hope that helps with your school project," the professor said. "But if you need more, you should check out the Underground Tour. My great-aunt loved history, so she volunteered there for years after she retired. Maybe you can learn more about the book there."

Nomi perked up—they had a direction again, a next step in their hunt—but she caged her hope. "Why would we learn about the book there?"

Nomi had never done the Underground Tour, but most Seattleites knew about it. It was a tour through the tunnels beneath the streets of Seattle. A city that, once, hundreds of years ago, had burned to ash.

"Well, I know she donated some of her collection to the tour company. And this book is from that time period." Professor Newman turned the journal over and pointed to a tiny indentation on the back cover. "See? Stone and Taylor Printing and Binding Company. It was one of the first printing companies when colonists settled here."

Nomi had never paid much attention to the logo, but now she saw the stamped initials: S&T.

"If you want to learn more about something, you have to learn where it comes from—and *when* it comes from. You have to learn which ring of memory it sits in, so to speak. Then you can learn its secrets."

Nomi shivered. *The book's secrets.*

Professor Newman tapped the logo. "And see? Here's something interesting. We know this book was made in a specific time period, because this company was only in operation from 1876 to 1889—right before a very important moment in Seattle history. Right before the Seattle fire."

WHAT DO TREES KNOW OF FIRE?

It starts with drought, a lack of rain that leaves our bark dry and our branches brittle. But it's heat, really, that does it—that inescapable pressure, that thickness in the air, the kind of heat that mounts and mounts until only a spark will satisfy it.

We know that heat. We know those summers. And during one of those summers, on the corner of First and Madison, a girl stepped into a cabinet shop with a tree clutched to her chest and ink tucked in her pockets.

It had been years since she'd gotten those first two journals, and she'd gathered wisdom diligently, filling an entire notebook as the world changed around her. She'd believed, at first, that everyone would live together on this land. But with each day, more and more settlers arrived, and peace seemed less and less possible.

By the time she started the second notebook, some of her father's friends had rioted, pushing Chinese immigrants onto boats, forcing them out of the country. Others had set fire to Duwamish longhouses, destroying entire villages in the process. Tension rippled in the streets, almost as hot as the air itself.

Still, the girl continued her project. In the cabinet shop, she asked a young man working in the back if he had time to take a break.

He was new to this continent and eager to help, so he left a pot of glue on the stove and walked over.

Do you have any advice? she asked.

He'd heard of her project—this strange girl who asked everyone she saw for a piece of themselves, and he searched his memory, drudging up some long-forgotten wisdom and translating it from Norwegian into fractured English: *Time is a circle.*

(We trees thought: *Welllll, time is a* ring. *But close enough.*)

What does that mean? she asked.

He explained: *The past is a lesson. What happened before will repeat, so we must learn from it.*

(*Welllll,* we trees thought again, *it won't* repeat, *but it will speak, chattering to the future like morning birds on branches.*)

Think of a tree: each new ring built around the past. Without the sturdy core of all that came before, a tree would collapse.

But human historians are never as sophisticated as trees. Their lifespans are too short to see the forest. So, sure, time is a circle. Close enough.

Thanking him, she left, another seed collected, and he went back to sanding cedar.

He forgot about the glue pot.

It ignited just hours later—a spark that set a timber city ablaze.

ARTHUR

THE WHOLE TREE THING TOTALLY FREAKED ARTHUR out. He couldn't stop thinking about it, even two days later.

It wasn't Nomi's fault. Obviously. But it kinda felt that way. Because every time she got involved in his life, he started thinking about things he'd rather not think about.

Like how trees felt pain—not really but *kind of.* Ugh.

It wasn't like Arthur was some monster who hated trees. It was more like . . . how could anyone live with that information? How could they know that and carry on during a forest fire like everything was normal?

"She's not normal," Lucas said.

Arthur hadn't been listening, and for a strange moment he thought Lucas had reached into his brain and pulled out Nomi.

But Lucas was talking about Vi.

"She's surprising," he continued. "She's, like, real."

They were sitting in Lucas's backyard after cross-country practice because, despite the smoke, it was still better than sitting inside where Lucas's parents might overhear.

On a non-hazy day, Lucas's house, perched at the very top of Queen Anne hill, had an incredible view of the city—which made sense because everything about Lucas's house was incredible. Lucas's dad was high up at Google, and his mom was from Singapore and had a bunch of family money.

Lucas was rich enough to spend winter breaks in the Bahamas and eat sushi once a week and even to turn the basement into his own state-of-the-art gaming room, which made Arthur kinda jealous, but whatever. At least Lucas let him play.

Arthur looked out at the city and found nothing but gray. Practice had been moved to the indoor track today, and now Arthur understood why. Just sitting outside, the smoke made his throat itch.

The air would be like this as long as the forest kept burning, which meant the air would be like this until it rained.

And this time of year, Seattle could go weeks without rain.

If trees could feel pain—

Lucas was looking at him expectantly, and Arthur still hadn't been listening.

"Yeah . . ." Arthur said, totally lost. "I guess."

"Vi's wearing different clothes now," Lucas continued. "And you know what that means."

"Oh." Arthur's stomach twisted. Was he supposed to know? "Sure."

"She wants attention," Lucas explained.

If Arthur was a better person, he might have said something else. Like, stand up for Vi or something. He was never as close to her as he was to Nomi, but they'd still been friends. Except, what was he supposed to say?

Lucas snorted. "Who knows? Maybe something will happen at the dance next week. Thanks for talking me up to her, by the way."

"What?"

"She said you told her I was cool."

"Oh . . ." Arthur had the feeling he'd done something wrong, which was ridiculous, because Lucas *was* cool.

Lucas leaned back. "You're lucky you don't have to think about all this girl stuff."

"What?" Arthur asked, before remembering that Lucas thought he was gay. "Oh, no, I'm not—"

The back door swung open, and Lucas's dad walked out with a tray full of raw steaks. Arthur tried not to notice that they were bleeding.

"I see you two are enjoying the great weather," he joked, gesturing to the smoke.

"Nah, just avoiding you," Lucas responded.

Lucas's dad laughed. Lucas laughed. Arthur could never tell if they liked each other or hated each other. He laughed too.

Lucas's dad lit a match, and Arthur watched it flicker before he tossed it onto the grill.

Lucas raised his brows. "You're cooking?"

"Grilling isn't cooking." He turned to Arthur and held up the tray of oozing red steaks. "Scared?"

Arthur pushed out a single *ha*. "Of great food?"

He'd eaten meat before, but his dads were vegetarians, so all the meals they made were meatless. They said once that over eight hundred million trees were cut down in the Amazon to raise cattle and, like, great, there was another thought that wouldn't leave Arthur's brain. He tried not to feel guilty.

Lucas's dad turned to his son. "If your mom keeps getting on me about cooking more, she's gonna have to deal with steak every night."

"Fine by me," Lucas said.

"Well, don't say that in front of her, or she'll think she won." Lucas's dad laughed again. Lucas laughed again.

Arthur felt a little sick—maybe it was the smoke? He wished they would go inside.

"Your mom's got all these ideas in her head nowadays," Lucas's dad went on.

Arthur had the very strong feeling that he shouldn't be part of this conversation.

Lucas rolled his eyes. "Yeah, Dad, we wouldn't want Mom thinking for herself."

"You joke about this now." His dad slapped a steak on the grill. "But this is serious stuff. I wish we didn't have to talk about this, but kids are getting dragged into too much nonsense these days."

"Arthur loves nonsense," Lucas joked.

Arthur grimaced. He had no clue what Lucas meant.

"I'm serious." Lucas's dad turned to them, letting the steaks sizzle behind him. "I hope things will balance out again, but girls have all the power now. They get opportunities just for being girls, and they can make up anything to ruin your lives."

"We'll try not to have our lives ruined, Dad." Lucas's voice dripped with sarcasm, but he leaned forward, just a little.

"You can't say it, especially not in this city, but it's true," his dad went on. "It's harder than ever to be a boy. At least you'll get the benefits of being Asian, Lucas—I still worry, but people aren't as prejudiced against them as they are against white boys."

For a second, Arthur thought Lucas looked annoyed, or even hurt. But then he grinned and ran a hand through his hair, all mocking suave. "Lucky me."

His dad grinned, half scolding. "Now, now, don't abuse it."

Arthur really, truly could not tell if they were joking.

Lucas's dad turned back to Arthur. "But take it from me, the world's rough out there."

Arthur swallowed. That, at least, felt true. He saw comments online sometimes—*all guys are terrible* and *men are the worst*—that was prejudice, right? Whatever, he hated the way it made him feel. Like he'd done something wrong before he'd even done anything at all.

He could never talk to his dads about that, though. What would he tell them? That it was hard sometimes? That would be embarrassing, and probably wrong somehow.

"I'm sorry you're growing up in this time, I really am. Honestly . . ." Lucas's dad gestured to the sky above them. "Our generation failed you."

Arthur shifted in his seat. His dads sometimes said something similar—*we adults have failed*—and like, cool, thanks, what was Arthur supposed to do with that?

Lucas and his dad slid into talking about the Seahawks, which was simple and easy, so Arthur tuned out until the steaks were ready.

Then he and Lucas grabbed their plates and disappeared into the windowless, air-conditioned basement, with the giant TV and plush couches, where they could eat their meat and shoot some zombies in peace.

It was fun and light and easy, and that was all Arthur wanted.

For a few hours, he could turn off his brain, and he didn't have to worry about trees or smoke or the world-turned-rough. And the steak tasted good, as long as he didn't think about it.

VI

THE DRESSES WERE BECOMING HEAVY.

Vi was already carrying five, but she'd wandered through the store to grab a sixth, because suddenly her clothes felt wrong on her body, and it was like she was floating outside herself, looking down, seeing all her flaws.

She grabbed another dress and wove through the racks, back toward her mom. But then she slowed. A white woman with wispy brown hair was approaching her mom, and Vi sensed that whatever was about to happen, she wasn't supposed to hear it.

So, of course, Vi busied herself with a rack close enough to eavesdrop.

"I know this isn't my business," the woman said, voice low, "and I'm sorry to bother you, but I just have to say, I filed my adoption paperwork last week, which I've been so nervous about, and seeing you and your daughter together made me feel a lot better. What a beautiful family."

For a second Vi was confused, but the second was too

brief, and then she understood. She was Asian, and her mom was not.

She was suddenly aware of how the dress hangers dug into her arm.

Her mother's smile froze at an odd angle. "Oh. I don't know what—"

"Gosh, I know, I'm sorry." The other woman threw her hands up and smiled sheepishly. "I shouldn't make a big deal out of it. I hate when people make a big deal out of it."

"Right." Her mom's smile began to fall, and for a wild moment Vi wanted to catch it. But her hands were full of dresses.

She meant to turn around and walk away, but her body had other ideas, because somehow her legs propelled her toward her mom. "I'm ready," she announced, gesturing to her heap of fabric.

She needed the conversation to end, so she could try on the clothes, and pick a dress, and the hangers wouldn't dig so deep anymore.

"Oh hi!" The woman's smile grew larger as she looked at Vi. "You are so pretty."

"Thank you." Vi didn't know what else to say.

Her mom seemed to remember herself. She put her hand on Vi's back, and her voice grew clipped. "My daughter and I are going to try on dresses now. Goodbye."

She took some of the dresses from Vi's hands, lightening the load, and whisked her into the dressing room.

"Mom." Vi hesitated. "Are you okay?"

Her mom looked like she wanted to say something, but then she grabbed Vi's shoulders and kissed the top of her head three times. "Of course," she said. "Now go try on some dresses and make me cry because my baby's growing up too fast."

Vi forced a laugh before escaping into the dressing room.

Why was her pulse still racing? It was silly, really, because nothing had even *happened*. A stranger had gotten confused. That was it.

She tried on the first dress. Horrible.

She tried the second. Even worse.

On the third, her eyes began to water. Why did she look so wrong?

She'd thrown out most of her old clothes that summer, in a desperate attempt to *fit* herself better. And for a little while it had worked. But now the new clothes felt wrong too.

She sat on the dressing room chair and tried to breathe. Without meaning to, she reached for her phone, letting her fingers find Instagram.

Her mom's post was only forty-three seconds old:

A rare photo of all four of them, smiling at the beach. Vi remembered that trip to the Oregon coast. She'd gotten a sunburn so sharp and hot she'd cried. But this photo was before all that.

Mixed families, can you relate? the caption read. *I love my beautiful family so much it hurts, but I hate that some people can't see us clearly. A woman today assumed my flower was adopted, because how could my daughter possibly be Asian? I was rude, I admit. I ended the conversation quickly. But maybe I should've said more. Maybe I should've educated her. Did I handle it right? I don't know. Sometimes I don't know if I'm doing right by my daughters. All I can do is hope my best is good enough.*

Vi read and reread the caption. She looked at the closed door. It was quiet outside, and Vi felt like she'd discovered a private universe, a hidden mom, with secrets that weren't Vi's to know or savor.

Except it wasn't secret, of course, because it belonged to the whole world.

And then came the comments, always so many, always so fast, rushing in over the post like smoke over a city. Lots of supportive, heart-filled comments, sure. But also: *Why do you have to make everything about race?* And also: *Adopted families are families too.* And also: *Mixed babies are the prettiest!*

A knock sounded at the dressing-room door. "Violet, sweet? Any contenders?"

"Um . . ." Vi worked to steady her voice. "Not really. I'm still changing."

"All right!" Her mom's voice sounded like a lie, and Vi wondered if her own voice sounded the same. "Just show me when you're ready, okay?"

Vi mumbled a yes, but she couldn't speak anymore. If she did, the words would catch in her throat and catapult into a sob, and she wasn't interested.

Nomi. She had to tell Nomi.

But when Vi pulled up her messages, she hesitated.

Nomi would care a whole lot. Which was great. She'd be mad at this woman, which would be nice. But she wouldn't *really* understand.

Nomi knew a whole lot, but sometimes she didn't notice the same things Vi did. Like, once when they were walking downtown, Nomi commented on how unfair it was that so many people couldn't afford homes. Nomi was right, and Vi hadn't thought about it like that until Nomi said it. But then, Nomi hadn't seemed to notice that most of those people weren't white. That was also unfair, which seemed obvious to Vi.

It freaked Vi out a little, the way two people could look at the world and see totally different things, even when those two people were best friends.

Her thumb tapped Lucas's name instead.

Something happened, she wrote.

She typed more and deleted and typed and deleted, and his response came as she was trying to find the words.

> you always delete your messages before you send them. im not gonna judge if theres typos.

Embarrassment rose in her throat and hung there in a tight little ball. She felt caught. **Lol ok**, she wrote. **But what if I say something dumb?**

She sent it.

And he replied, **then itll be our secret.**

Vi stared at that message for a long time. She knew, logically, that he didn't mean anything that deep by it. But . . . still. What would a shared secret with Lucas taste like? Cinnamon, maybe. Or, no. There was something more, something about this secret that burned.

She typed all of it, everything, about *Raising Wildflowers,* and the wispy-haired white woman, and the Instagram comments, and how she didn't know why all this mattered to her, except that sometimes she felt like she was split down the middle, half-and-half, and she never knew what people were seeing when they looked at her.

As she typed, she felt lighter. Maybe, maybe she could unload some of the weight that had settled in her chest.

When she was done, before she could regret it, before she could apologize for it all, Lucas wrote back. Just three words. And they were exactly the right ones.

> i get it.

NOMI

DESPITE THE SMOKE, THICK AS EVER, NOMI AND VI were sitting under their oak tree during lunch period, because that was where they always ate.

"Don't you get it?" Nomi asked. "If I invite Arthur today, then it's weird. But now it's also weird *not* to invite him. Right? Because he kind of involved himself in this whole thing. And he *was* kind of helpful with the professor. I mean, he asked some good questions. It almost seemed like he cared. Do you think he cares? Why would he care? Not that *I* care."

She was overthinking it. She knew that. But it had been a week since they saw the professor, and they'd only just secured a slot on an Underground Tour, and Nomi was feeling antsy.

The book was old, apparently. 1800s old. Which meant the author was no longer alive. Which was fine, of course, because they had a lead on where to find the sequel, and Nomi was closer to the next book than she'd ever been. But that length of time—*hundreds of years!*—made the sequel feel further away. How had the first book made its way from the 1800s to the Museum of Lost and Found? How many people had held it and read it before her? And if people had been reading it for hundreds of years, how did it still feel so specific to her, like it was hers and hers alone?

Okay, well, Vi's and Arthur's, too.

"Sure," Vi said to her phone as she typed something Nomi couldn't read.

"Sure what?" Nomi said. "I asked like seventeen questions."

"Oh, I mean sure you should invite him." Vi kept typing.

Ever since Vi got a phone last year, she'd been distracted by it. Most times, Nomi tried to ignore it. But sometimes she wanted to take Vi's phone and throw it into Lake Washington.

With a great deal of restraint, Nomi asked, "What are you looking at?"

Vi glanced up, startled, like she'd entirely forgotten about Nomi's existence. "My phone," she said, which was not a satisfying answer. It chirped, but she slid it into her backpack before Nomi could see.

Nomi raised her brows, prompting, because apparently Vi had a secret, and it was Nomi's best-friend responsibility to know it. "Violet Noelle Sun Ja Kim!"

Vi wrapped her arms around her bag. "Nomi Hastings," she replied, which was still not an answer.

"Who are you texting?" As Nomi asked, her mind supplied *Arthur*—and why did that make her sick to her toes?

But Vi took the world's deepest breath and said, "Lucas."

The way she said it made everything inside Nomi, all the parts of her that always raced, freeze. Maybe it shouldn't have been a big deal that Vi had a crush—Nomi and Vi had talked about crushes before. But they'd always been harmless. Distant. And this felt different, because Vi didn't say his name like an answer. She said his name like a *possibility*.

Nomi hadn't even considered the possibility of possibilities.

She swallowed, focusing on the problem at hand. "Lucas is the reason Arthur stopped being friends with us," she said.

Vi peered at her. "That's interesting, because you always said *Arthur* was the reason Arthur stopped being friends with us."

Nomi's cheeks got hot. Vi was right. Why was Nomi making excuses for Arthur? "Well, yeah, I know. But it's not a coincidence."

This conversation was running away from her, and she wasn't quite sure where it was headed. "Okay, well, remember last year when Ms. Grange assigned me to sit next to Lucas and Gregory?" she pushed, trying to get things back on track.

Vi nodded, "And you thought they were distracting."

"Yeah, and . . ."

Nomi hadn't told anyone why, not even Vi.

But one day Alice Thorton, a girl in their class, had walked up to ask Ms. Grange a question. She was wearing a long white skirt, and Nomi had watched as Lucas's and Gregory's eyes followed her.

Even then, something in Nomi had turned gray. First she'd thought, *Nobody will ever look at me like that.* Then she'd thought, *Maybe they will.* She wasn't sure which was worse, and that was unsettling, because she hated being unsure.

And then Lucas had whispered to Gregory, loud enough for Nomi to hear: *You can see through her skirt.*

Under the tree, Nomi reached for words. "He's just . . ."

Back in the classroom, her heart had drummed in her ears, so loudly she couldn't hear her thoughts. She'd turned to look—she couldn't help it—and seen that Lucas was lying. Alice's skirt wasn't see-through, which was almost worse. Lucas was lying just because he could, as if his words could reshape reality.

After that, Nomi's palms would sweat every time she sat down at her desk. Every day, she thought about asking her teacher to switch seats. But every day, she said nothing. She refused to be a problem kid. She didn't have that luxury, not when her grades determined her scholarship. So she did her work and got good grades until, eventually, the seating assignment changed again.

"He's just . . ." Now Nomi searched for the right word and found only imperfect ones. "Bad."

"He's not *bad*," Vi insisted.

Nomi nodded. "Okay . . . but . . . he's not *good*."

"Seriously, Nomi?"

"He said something gross to Gregory! About a girl!"

Vi faltered, blinking. Then she inhaled sharply. "Do

you have to be so black-and-white about everything? Have you thought about it from his perspective? Whatever he said, he probably didn't mean it. He was probably just trying to make friends, and that's how guys make friends with Gregory, unfortunately."

Nomi tried not to think of Arthur, and failed. Was that the kind of stuff he'd said to make friends with Lucas and Gregory? "Right, yeah, but isn't someone who wants to be friends with Gregory automatically suspicious?"

Vi sighed. "You're too hard on people, Nomi. We can't all be you."

Nomi's stomach swooped. Fact: When blood flowed to the legs, in preparation to run, the stomach reacted with a swooping feeling. But knowing that didn't make her feel better, not when Vi was looking at her like that. "What's that supposed to mean?"

Vi hesitated. "Nothing."

Nomi knew a lot, and she knew now that she was walking on a tightrope. She knew that the fall was far, so far she couldn't see the bottom.

"Okay, maybe you're right," she said, though she only half believed it. "Maybe he's not that bad."

Vi pressed her lips into a tighter line. Apparently, that was not good enough.

"Maybe he's *fine*!" Nomi relented. "Maybe even . . . okay?"

Vi narrowed her eyes, and Nomi felt a little dizzy until Vi laughed. "You are trying so hard to be nice about Lucas."

"So hard!" Nomi shouted, throwing her arms wide to convey the breadth of her effort.

Vi nudged her. "I'll settle for okay," she said, and Nomi started to relax again. She leaned back against the tree trunk. Above them, the branches swayed softly, green against gray. It almost sounded like they were whispering.

Then Vi whispered, even softer, "I'm scared he won't like me."

"If he doesn't like you, he has no brain."

Vi snorted. "You can't say he has no brain."

"Fine," Nomi conceded. "If he doesn't like you, he is a pig brain."

Vi considered this. "Pigs are smarter than dogs."

Nomi grinned. They were back to Vi and Nomi, and this was fun. "Okay, a chicken brain." She paused. "Actually, I think chickens are pretty smart. They talk to one another in their own language."

"Oh . . ." Vi frowned. "A pelican brain?"

"That's good," Nomi said, though she knew nothing about pelicans. "That's what he would be if he didn't like you."

Vi laughed. "Thanks," she said. "I know it's silly, but I keep thinking he might ask me to the dance."

"Oh." Nomi tried to keep the lightness, but gravity shifted, and suddenly she felt heavy. She'd barely thought about the fundraising dance. Tickets were a hundred dollars, and even though the scholarship students got free entry, it still felt weird to Nomi. Like everyone else there could afford that much for one night, and they didn't have to think about it. "We're going to that?"

"Yeah? I mean, *I* am."

"Oh," Nomi repeated. "Well, then I am too."

Except, if Vi was going with Lucas, there wouldn't be any room for Nomi. She would be alone. Not like no date alone, but no *friends* alone, which was about fifteen thousand times worse.

The bell rang, but neither of them stood. Nomi looked at her best friend. Beneath the new pink, the new heels, the new name, she was still the girl Nomi had known for years, and despite the laughter and the pelicans, Nomi still had the itchy feeling that she was missing something. "Is there something more going on with Lucas?" she asked. "Something you're not telling me?"

For a moment Vi hesitated. But then she reached over to squeeze Nomi's hand. "There's nothing else to say," she promised.

So Nomi forced the worry living between her shoulder blades to unknot. Vi was telling the truth. A best friend always knew.

ARTHUR

ARTHUR KNEW TWO THINGS: (1) HIS NOMI PROBLEM would only get worse the more he saw her. And (2) He didn't want to stop seeing her.

She'd approached him in the hallway after lunch that afternoon—when he wasn't with Lucas or any of his cross-country friends.

"I've secured Vi, my mom, and me a spot on the Underground Tour this evening," she'd said. "You can come if you want. But don't feel obliged."

As usual, Arthur had no idea why Nomi used such big words. And, as usual, he found himself wanting more of them.

What a mess.

Calamity, as Nomi might say.

And because he could not resist her, he found himself sitting in the waiting room of Seattle's Underground Tour with Nomi, Vi, Danthony, and Nomi's mom—even though he'd done the tour twice already, with both sets of grandparents.

Nomi looked even more *Nomi* than usual today. Her wild hair frizzed around her face, and she wore all black like a burglar, and her right leg kept tapping, then her left, then her right.

Arthur's gaze drifted to her again and again as they waited for their tour guide.

"What?" Nomi asked, when their eyes met for the third time.

"Nothing." Arthur snapped his gaze back to his feet. His shoes were dirty. Should he get new shoes for the dance? Not that he was planning to go. Obviously.

"Okaaaaay." Nomi glanced at the parents, who stood a few dozen feet away, talking about whatever parents talked about, and lowered her voice. "We should learn what we can from this tour, but let's stay focused. We need to find out everything we can about Stone and Taylor Printing and the prophecy books and maybe Professor Newman's great-aunt."

Vi nodded. "Professor Newman said her great-aunt volunteered here, so she might've been friends with our guide."

Arthur realized they were looking at him, waiting for some kind of contribution. "Right," he said.

Something about Nomi sucked up all of Arthur's attention, which was unpleasant, but now Vi made him uncomfortable too, because what was he supposed to do with the stuff Lucas had said?

"Hello, hello, hello!" A tall, college-age person with curly brown hair, pale skin, and a velvet green cape burst into the small room. "The moment you've all been waiting for has arrived! The name's Zed, they/them pronouns."

Arthur looked around, wondering who Zed could possibly be talking to, until he realized, right, duh, the tour was starting. And they were the only ones on it.

"I like history, fire, and avoiding the sun," Zed continued, "which makes me perfect for this job, if I do say so myself. So, fear not! I will be your great guide through the underworld—I mean, underground—" They paused for laughter, and grinned when the parents eagerly *obliged*. "Cool, cool. That doesn't always get laughs. I can tell we're gonna get along."

Arthur glanced back at Danthony, who gave him two thumbs up, and suddenly he wished the group were much larger. His dad was way too happy about Arthur spending time with Nomi and Vi again, and though Danthony was carefully *not bringing it up*, Arthur could feel the joy radiating off him.

Zed led them down a few city blocks until they reached an iron gate. "At least the smoke's less bad down here," they said, and as the group descended, the world grew darker, colder, smaller.

This felt different from the other times he'd taken the tour. Before, it had just been a cheesy tourist attraction. But Nomi made it feel like something more—like they were stepping into the city's secrets.

Nomi followed right behind Zed, like she was the

assistant tour guide or something. Had she always moved this way? Like the world wasn't fast enough for her? Arthur was the runner here, yet he found himself struggling to keep up.

Zed walked them through the tunnels, the bones of a city that used to be. Small stained-glass windows let light into the cramped space, blacked out momentarily by people walking above them, oblivious to what lay beneath their feet.

"So where we're standing right now was actually downtown Seattle, over a hundred years ago," Zed explained. "After the Great Seattle Fire swept through the city, settlers raised the streets by twenty feet, and essentially rebuilt a whole new city on top of ash."

When he'd done the tour before, Arthur thought that was cool—like there was a secret world underground. But now it felt darker, a whole city built on top of destruction.

"What started the fire?" Nomi asked.

"Great question!" Zed exclaimed, like they really thought it was a *great* question. "We believe it started with a glue pot in a small cabinet shop. The glue was hot, a few rags caught fire, and the wooden cabinets went up in flames. It didn't take much. This whole place was a tinderbox, a lumber city made of wood."

Vi wrapped her arms around herself. "So are the tunnels . . . haunted?"

"Oh no. Nobody died in the fire!" Zed said. "So,

no ghosts, but I do believe spaces have auras. A place remembers."

The aura, to Arthur, was extremely creepy. He felt trapped. He needed to run.

"And the fire changed the shape of Seattle. When people rebuilt, they banned wood buildings downtown, only allowing brick."

They walked through the tunnels, and while Zed talked about what used to be, Arthur could only see what *was*, and what was . . . was nothing.

"And a bunch of settlers fought hard to rebuild *their* businesses only," Zed continued. "The wealthiest settlers used the new fear of fire as a weapon, slapping fire violations on businesses owned by Japanese immigrants and Indigenous folks. It put a lot of them out of work."

"That's a familiar story," Danthony chimed in.

And that was the kind of comment Arthur couldn't follow. It wasn't familiar to him, and he didn't feel like he was allowed to ask.

"Oh, totally," Zed agreed. "White men have made a whole lot of rules that benefit them, and harm everyone else."

Arthur felt the words like a weight in his stomach, and he turned to his dad, but Danthony just nodded along, like it wasn't personal.

But wasn't it? Because he was a white guy. He thought of what Lucas's dad had said—it *was* hard to be a boy, because it meant people blamed him for everything, even though he hadn't done *anything*. Then he felt bad for thinking that, because it seemed wrong, so he tried not to think anything at all.

Instead, he listened as Nomi asked more questions about Seattle history and the printing company and poetry and *did a lot of people journal back then?* and *did a lot of people read those journals?* and *what do you think about girls turning to flame?*

Zed entertained every one of her questions, but none of their answers seemed to satisfy her. This was why Arthur didn't get involved. Asking questions usually just led to more questions.

Finally they emerged back into the world above. It was thick with gray and ash, but at least they could see again.

As Zed led them back toward the Underground Tour headquarters, Nomi leaned over to whisper, "We still have to ask about the professor's aunt, but I didn't want to ask in front of the parents."

"I don't think Zed was friends with an old-lady volunteer," Arthur said.

Nomi shot him a look, and he tried not to think about what it meant. "You never know. Zed's very friendly."

They stopped in front of a large wooden pole carved with eagles and other animals. Arthur had walked by it a million times but never paid it much attention.

"And for our final stop," Zed announced, "here's a totem pole that settlers stole from the Tlingit people in Alaska and refused to give back. Which, speaking of stealing, reminds me to tell you that we are currently walking on land stolen from the Coast Salish peoples."

Arthur looked at his dirty shoes.

That weight in his stomach turned to nausea—a sick, dizzy feeling, like he didn't know where to step.

"I gotta be careful about which groups I say that to," Zed added. "Some people write bad reviews when you say too much truth."

Danthony coughed to cover a laugh, and Nomi's mom snapped her fingers to say *yes!* in that dorky adult way. Zed saluted them, then led them back to where they'd started: a small room with a check-in, some chairs, and a collection of faded photographs.

"You've been great," Zed said, before disappearing into a room marked EMPLOYEES ONLY. And, just like that, the tour was over.

Nomi's mom smiled at the kids. "Got what you needed?"

Vi and Arthur exchanged a look, because no, it wasn't what they needed, and it *definitely* wasn't what Nomi needed.

"Uh . . ." Arthur glanced at Nomi. "Is that it?"

Nomi didn't respond. She was looking, very intently, at the employees-only door. She sucked her teeth. Then she walked right up to that door and pushed it open.

"Nomi!" her mom cried.

"Don't worry, Ms. Hastings," Vi said, sounding way older than she was. "Let me handle it."

And then Vi went hurrying off after Nomi, and Arthur wasn't gonna just *stand* there like a nobody, so he hurried after Vi, and then all three of them were stumbling into what turned out to be an oversized closet with a desk stuffed inside.

Zed sat at the desk, phone in one hand, a tuna sandwich in the other.

"Hey," they said, slowly setting the tuna down. "Is there a problem? Was it the totem pole?"

"Oh, no, that was super interesting," Nomi said. "We just have more questions."

"Sorry to bother you," Vi added.

"Yes, sorry." Nomi pulled the book of predictions out of her backpack. "See, I was asking about all that because we found this book that tells the future—"

"For school," Arthur interrupted.

"Yeah, for school," Nomi finished.

Zed frowned. "If you stole a teacher's grade book or something, I should . . . probably tell your parents?"

"No, no!" Nomi said. "We are not delinquents."

Zed's frown deepened. "Um."

Somehow, Nomi always sounded like she was lying.

Arthur took the book from Nomi's hands and opened it, holding the looping handwriting up for Zed to see. "No, really. It's a super old book of, like, poetry, or"—he glanced at Nomi—"something."

"And that's why we're here," Nomi said, gathering steam again, "because a professor at the university told us that this notebook was created during the era of the Seattle fire, which you know a lot about, and the professor's great-aunt used to work here, and maybe donated more stuff to your records? Like another book! One that looks exactly like this one! For example."

Zed leaned over to inspect the book, and Arthur found himself holding his breath. Not that he cared. But, like, if they found the sequel, it'd be cool.

Zed nodded, hair bouncing. "I totally see why you like this thing. But we don't keep a bunch of donations like that. Everything we have is in this little gift-shop museum. The rest of it . . . gets trashed."

Nomi choked on an *oh*, and Arthur waited for her to say more, but she didn't. Was she about to cry? Arthur really, really didn't want her to cry. He looked at Vi, waiting for her to make Nomi feel better, but she just looked stunned. He pictured the second book, tossed into a bin with greasy burger wrappers—

"But if it wasn't," he blurted. "Trashed, I mean. Where would it go?"

"Look at you, little go-getters." Zed nodded approvingly as they considered the question. "Well, there's the Seattle Room in the main branch of the public library. Old maps, letters, tons of books. I don't know about your poetry book, but sometimes we send stuff there."

"That's perfect," Vi said.

"Good!" Zed looked relieved. "Stay in school, or whatever inspirational thing adults are supposed to say to kids."

"Thanks, Zed." Nomi came to life again. She smiled—

and when she turned to Arthur, he didn't know where to look, but he knew he felt wobbly.

This was not a good feeling, and he didn't want to stop feeling it.

He looked at the floor. He didn't know where to step.

HUMANS DON'T PAY MUCH ATTENTION TO THE UNDERground.

Our roots dig deep. They connect us, sustain us, and anchor us to the Earth, and human roots are much the same—but some people will live whole lives without knowing their roots exist.

In 1938, a twelve-year-old Japanese boy worked in a hotel on Second and Madison, just a block from where a glue pot caught fire forty years before. But he wasn't worried about those roots, nor the ones that led him back to Japan. To him, history was decades old and stale, and he cared more about his parents' business.

He helped them clean out the rooms and paint and update the VACANCY sign, but his family still struggled. Business was bad. The Depression had hit hard, and his wealthy neighbors only made life harder by marking them with fire violations, as if his Japanese blood itself were a fire hazard.

On the worst days, he felt like it might be. On the days

when he felt this world was not built for him, when the rules of who and how to be were hard to know and even harder to follow, when he felt like everyone else was seeing him through water, an image warped and warbled, there was something in him that wanted to burn. He hid that flame like a secret, glowing brighter and brighter—

Until he found a pair of books. Old journals, written in blue ink. He was cleaning out room 208 one day and there they were, waiting for him, almost like they knew he was ready.

Right away, he could tell there was something special about the books. The phrases were strange, sometimes nonsensical, but as soon as he read them, it was like they were his.

He absorbed the words, tasting them, and they set fire in his bones.

Time is a circle.

What's yours is mine, too much to take.

A taste of something new, and something blue.

With all his extra coins, he bought a can of blue paint, and he updated the hotel sign in fresh color. He left VA-CANCY in big, bold letters, but beneath it, he added a new phrase from the book every week, painting and re-painting, translating the words, Japanese and English side by side.

When he ran out of the book's words, he wrote his own. First on the sign, then into the second book.

He started with this: *Seeing is a flower.*

It was something his mother said—a root of his own, a reworking of the Japanese proverb, which translated into English as *Not seeing is a flower.*

His parents had different interpretations of the proverb, but his mom took it as, *The perfection of imagination is more beautiful than reality. Some things are better left unseen.*

His mom disagreed.

Back in Japan, she'd been an artist who specialized in kintsugi, a form of pottery that made beauty out of broken bits. She, too, saw the world at a slant.

To experience the world as it is, to refuse to run from it, that is true beauty, she insisted. *Seeing is a flower.*

Nearly one hundred years later, another sign with the same words will stand in the same city.

Does it matter? If time is a circle, then what is the point of roots? What is the point of history? Maybe this is just a coincidence.

But if time is a ring, each moment containing the past, nestled into memory, fitting just right, then perhaps we must listen.

Time is a ring, with something to say.

Time is a ring.

And it's calling.

VI

AFTER THE TOUR, AFTER DINNER, IN THE PRIVACY OF her bed and the dark, Vi pulled out her phone and scrolled through the Instagram account. Seeing her family through all these strangers' eyes, reading the comments about her life, searching for herself in all those images of herself—it had become impossible to resist.

And tonight, it was like she was seeing herself not only through Instagram strangers' eyes, but through the past and future, too. Her thoughts kept drifting to the burning city that existed and then, just as quickly, didn't. A ghost city without any ghosts.

Those people, all those years ago, did they taste secrets too? Did they hold each secret to their lips like a favorite ingredient? There was so much she didn't know about them, and so much that a kid a hundred years in the future wouldn't know about her. In a hundred years, nobody would know or care that her heart had stumbled when she texted a boy, or that she used to play piano and was almost good at it, or that sometimes she felt like she was seeing herself through a veil of smoke.

Was there a point to a secret self if nobody ever knew? If a tree fell in a forest and no one ever saw, did that tree really exist at all?

She turned off her phone. It was already past midnight, but she couldn't sleep, so she slid out of bed and headed to the bathroom, planning to warm her face with water and trick herself into exhaustion—but as she passed her sister's bedroom, a voice stopped her.

"Violet?"

Her name, in her sister's mouth, was enough to pull Vi out of her own head. She paused and pushed the cracked door open. "It's late," she whispered. "Why are you up?"

Blue peeked her small head out from under the covers. "Why are *you*?"

"Couldn't sleep."

"Clearly."

Vi tiptoed over to Blue and slid into her twin bed. Blue and their mom had painted the walls with color and shapes and squiggles and hung bright art that was so entirely *Blue*, but before that, the room had been Vi's, and though it was smaller than her new one, she missed it. The window was perfectly placed for the moon to reach in and kiss her night-pale skin.

"Are you scared of the dark?" Blue asked. "I know that used to scare you."

"What? No." Vi hadn't been scared of the dark in years. How did Blue even remember that?

"If you say so." Blue rolled over to face Vi. "You just looked scared."

Vi pushed some of the hair off her sister's forehead. "I guess. Maybe a little. But not of the dark. Of . . ." She had no idea how to explain what she was thinking about. "Big-kid stuff."

Blue snorted. "You're not *that* big."

"Maybe not," Vi said. "But I'm a lot bigger than you."

Blue stuck her tongue out, and it was so little-sisterly that suddenly Vi wanted to hold Blue in amber, to keep her from growing up.

"You could test your smoke alarm," Blue suggested.

"To *sleep*?"

"Well, you wouldn't fall asleep while it's on. But after. When you know you're safe."

Blue curled into the crook of Vi's arm, and Vi's heart pinched. She'd taken the batteries out of her smoke alarm after the fourth time Blue tested it, but she wasn't about to say that.

"And you could come up with a disaster plan," Blue continued. "I have an escape plan for every room in the house. In my room: run to Mom and Dad's room and climb down their balcony. In your room: go out the window, down the trellis, and around the back. In the kitchen—"

"Thanks, Blue," Vi interrupted. "You know, maybe Dad's right. Maybe you shouldn't be talking about all this in school."

"We don't really," Blue said. "We had a fire-safety day with Smokey Bear. But now I just research that stuff on my own, during library."

"Oh geez, Blue," Vi whispered. "Please stop doing that."

Blue yawned, deep and long. Her voice blurred with sleep. "How?"

"Um, maybe just read fun books during library?" Vi didn't know if that was good advice, but it didn't seem to matter because soon enough, Blue's breath turned to snores.

Here was this huge world, on fire, and here was Blue, curled up, safe enough to sleep. *How?*

Vi stayed there, listening, debating sleeping in this small bed with her small sister, but she didn't fit.

Slowly, silently, she stepped out and returned to her own room. After the color of Blue's room, Vi's white walls felt wrong. And now every other piece of her room did too. The window didn't face the moon. The gauzy curtains were too delicate. The canopy over her bed, which she'd begged her parents for, which had made her feel so pretty and princessy, was childish.

She got into bed and turned her phone back on. She should sleep—but sleep seemed so far, and she couldn't find a safe place, not like Blue had.

She pulled up her conversation with Lucas.

Their last exchange had been about cooking—Lucas was watching YouTube videos to learn how to cook. **itll be easier for my mom**, he'd written. And though he'd said nothing else, Vi could tell those words were precious, honest, hers.

Her fingers hovered over the keyboard. What would it be like, to dare to find a safe place in someone?

She thought of the digital billboard.

Seeing is a flower.

Online, she was trapped as that forever flower. Online, there were hundreds of thousands of her mom's followers, all those strangers, seeing. And there was a warped version of herself, a flower named Violet, being seen. Who were those people? Vi didn't know any of them. None of it was safe.

But what if someone could look at her and see more? Lucas had understood her when she'd told him about the shopping incident and her mom's Instagram.

He knew how she felt. He'd told her that his dad talked too much about things he didn't understand, and his mom never talked about anything real—but with Vi he could talk about everything. Their texts became a bubble, hidden from the rest of the world by a veil of smoke.

And in that bubble, he trusted her.

Now she wanted to trust him with the self that belonged to her and only her.

She clicked her lamp on.

In the mirror she could be pretty, maybe, at the right angles. She pulled her nightshirt off. Her hands were shaking now.

She tugged a plain bra on, wishing she had something

lacier, but she couldn't ask her mom for one. Imagine. It could end up on Instagram.

This would have to be enough. She would have to be enough. And the wild thing was, as she looked at herself in the mirror, preparing to do something she never thought she'd do, she believed that she *was* enough.

She took a photo. Winced. Weird face she was making.

Another photo. No. Why did her left eye always squinch when she smiled?

She stopped smiling. Another photo. No.

She flipped through Snapchat filters until she found the perfect one—not too obvious, but just right. It smoothed over the pimple on her chin and the blotchy redness on her cheeks. It made her eyes just a little bigger, rounder. Her nose thinner, sharper. She looked less like herself but maybe, in a weird way, more like herself, because she looked like the person she could one day become.

This wasn't a little flower. This was Vi.

She took a photo, and this one felt right. Her hands still shook. What would her mother think? And her mother's fans? And those hundred-years-from-now kids—if they could get past the outdated thing called Snapchat and the outdated thing called cell phones—would they understand this feeling, this thing inside her that wanted to burn?

But none of those people would ever see it. That was the point. This photo belonged to her and Lucas, a shared secret that tasted like honey.

Vi was a smart girl—even Nomi said so.

So she thought this through. She knew how to protect herself. She knew not to send the photo over text, where it could live forever. Snapchat would be fine.

In a different world, for a different girl, this could go terribly wrong. But here in this one, for her, she hoped it wouldn't.

She hoped. And she trusted. And she sent it.

PART III

What's yours is mine, too much to take.

NOMI

NOMI WAS A SMART GIRL, SO SHE UNDERSTOOD WHY one might question the book. She did too, at first.

She knew enough to be suspicious of anything that felt like wonder. She knew, too, how to do her research when the first inkling of *what if* tingled through her body. She knew that turning reality into magic had gotten humans into trouble throughout history.

Take the old witch trials, for example, where whole communities had burned women at the stake—turning girls to flame for talking too much, or not talking enough, or simply having a really nice garden.

Believing in magic was a dangerous, reckless thing, that was for sure.

But then came the book, with its consistent predictions that made the future knowable. It wasn't magic. Of course not. But what else was she supposed to call it?

Arthur was late to the library, but Nomi didn't mind. He was meeting her after his cross-country practice, and she'd been grateful to have some time after school for homework. Thinking about the book had been all-consuming, but she couldn't afford to let her grades slip, not with her scholarship, so she'd finished all her work, as meticulously and perfectly as possible, and now she was ready to search for the book without any distractions.

She bounced on her heels as she waited for him inside the library. The Central downtown branch was made of angles, the whole thing hanging on a tilt, and though Nomi knew there was math and science holding up the architecture, the walls still felt uncomfortably smashed together, off-kilter, like they could collapse at any moment.

The front doors slid open, and as soon as Arthur stepped in front of her, Nomi felt an illogical spike of nervousness. "Vi's busy," she blurted.

He pulled off his cloth mask. The smoke was even worse today, building and choking without any sign of rain. "Okay . . ."

"She had a dentist appointment that she really couldn't get out of." Nomi wasn't sure why she felt the need to explain. Vi herself hadn't explained this much to Nomi. She'd just said she had a dentist appointment and left it at that, as if it wouldn't matter. "I mean, she probably would've rescheduled, but her mom doesn't like to."

"So it's just . . . us?" He said this like it was the worst thing imaginable.

"You don't have to do this," she snapped. "I know you don't like me. I know you don't care about this. I know I'm the only one of us who actually needs to know—wants to know—"

"No, no, it's not that." He flushed. "I—you know. I want to be here."

Nomi blinked at him. "Oh. Well. Good."

They stared at each other, blink-blinking, and Nomi knew she was supposed to say something . . .

"That's cool," Arthur said, pointing over her shoulder.

Behind her was a wooden pole with carved animals and faces. A sign at its base read: ROTATING ART EXHIBIT. And then, in smaller font: STORY POLES—IN CONVERSATION WITH THE CITY. HISTORY WON'T BE FORGOTTEN.

"It's like the pole we saw on the Underground Tour," Arthur said.

"Kind of," Nomi agreed, though it wasn't quite. This one had a different energy. It felt raw.

He cleared his throat, like he was about to tell her something important. "Did you see the digital sign today? It changed. It's 'Ground from the Earth' now."

Nomi frowned. That was even worse than *Breathe* and *Seeing is a flower*. "That doesn't mean anything," she said. "All ground is from the earth."

"Right." Arthur looked back at the story pole, and Nomi

felt like she'd said something rude, which didn't make any sense, because she'd simply said something true.

And anyway, she shouldn't feel bad about what she said to Arthur. Right?

Nomi could not fathom why this was so awkward, but it was. "We don't have much time," she said finally.

Arthur nodded without meeting her eyes, and they took the elevator up to the Seattle Room on the top floor, getting closer and closer to the triangular ceiling. Above them, thick smoke pressed against the windows, giving the library an apocalyptic feel, like it might just be the last place on Earth.

No time to think about that.

"Excuse me!" Nomi stepped out of the elevator and rushed up to the librarian at the counter. "We're looking for the old letter archive. From the Seattle fire."

The librarian looked at them over his glasses. "Do you have an appointment?"

"Not officially." Not at all. Nomi chewed her cheek. She'd have to go home, make an appointment, and wait-wait-wait to turn to flame.

But the librarian smiled. "We'll make it work."

He led them into the stacks and handed them a box of latex gloves. "Wear these. If you rip or break anything, just tell me. I'm not that scary."

Nomi and Arthur donned their gloves, nodding obediently, and the librarian sat them at a small table beside a library cart stacked with metal boxes. Each box was labeled with a year.

"The professor said the journal was made between 1876 and 1889," Nomi said, already lifting the first box and dragging it over to the desk. It was heavier than it looked. "So, thirteen boxes."

"Fourteen," Arthur corrected before grimacing. "Sorry."

Nomi hated being wrong, and she expected to be annoyed, but she found she was just impressed. "Thanks. You're right."

Arthur fought back a smile, like she'd given him a gift, and Nomi felt a little glow in her chest. For some reason.

They got to work, sifting through the first box, then the second, then the third. Most of it was irrelevant—old accounting books, receipts, advertisements, housing documents—nothing remotely like the prophecies.

"What if it's not here?" Nomi murmured, more to herself than to Arthur.

"I mean . . ." Arthur looked up. "There's a lot that isn't here, right? Like, most of this stuff is just about people who could read or write in English, and could afford to buy things. There's a lot that's missing."

"Yeah, I guess so." Nomi swallowed. He was right again. Which was kind of terrible. "Keep looking, though."

Arthur kept his head down as he asked, "What are you gonna do with the book? When you find it?"

Nomi paused. "Do with it?"

"Yeah, like . . . are you gonna try to stop the prophecy from happening?"

She stared at him. No trace of sarcasm. But he had to know that she couldn't *prevent* the prophecies from coming true. Might as well try to prevent time from passing.

No, there was no adding to, or taking away, or changing those blue-inked pages. The only time she'd ever tried to prevent a prophecy was when it told her they'd stop being friends, and look how well *that* had turned out.

"What does it matter to you?" she bit out. "It's just a book, right? Isn't that what you said?"

He probably didn't even remember saying that, since he didn't seem to care about how he'd treated her at all, even a little. But color crept into his cheeks as he mumbled, "I shouldn't have said that."

Nomi had been spinning her anger into rage. She'd been ready to unleash it all. But hearing those words, the fight went out of her. "It's not only that you said that," she said quietly. "It's that you didn't say anything else. You stopped talking to us."

He winced. "Sorry."

"Well . . ." She'd imagined, many times before, telling Arthur exactly how angry she was. But she'd never imagined him *apologizing.* "Thanks for helping now."

He nodded, then buried himself back in history, letting his hair fall over his eyes as he looked through a box.

Now everything felt different to Nomi. The boy in front of her was no longer *Arthur, who'd wronged her.* But he wasn't quite *Arthur, whom she'd known for years,* either. He'd become a puzzle that she couldn't sort out. Which was completely uncharacteristic, because she was great at puzzles!

She focused on sorting through the years instead, losing herself in hundred-year-old paper, until—

"Hey, so I was wondering . . ." Arthur started.

Nomi brushed through a stack of crinkled love letters, the cursive wide and looping. "Yeah?"

"Um, well, you know the dance this weekend?"

She frowned. The *dance*? "Yeah, I know . . . the dance."

He probably wanted to ask Vi. Which made sense, of course. But then Nomi would have to tell him Vi liked someone else—except never mind, because she wasn't allowed to tell Arthur that Vi liked someone else, so she wouldn't be able to say anything.

"Right, so . . ." Arthur's voice cracked, and he went red when Nomi looked at him again.

She frowned. Was he really going to make her say it? It was fine if he liked Vi. It made Nomi's stomach twist in that unpleasant way, but still, it was fine. She didn't want to be the go-between, though.

They spoke at the same time.

"I can't talk about V—" she said.

"Are you going?" he asked, turning even redder.

She stared at him. *"Me?"*

"Never mind." Arthur turned back to 1883 and focused very intently on its contents, and Nomi felt her own cheeks heat, a rush and flush of sudden understanding.

He liked her. Her. Nomi. Fact?

She wanted to go back to talking about simple things, like predicting the future and turning to flame. "Um, yeah, I'm going to the dance," she said. "I don't really want to, but Vi does, so . . ."

"Oh, yeah, same," Arthur said quickly. "I mean, with Lucas. But since we're both going . . ."

He trailed off, as if he was about to ask her to the dance, and Nomi ran some mental calculations. None of this aligned with any gathered evidence whatsoever.

Unless . . .

A friendship ends with a crush, too much.

If *crush* didn't mean her own feelings were crushed, if it meant something else . . .

It felt so obvious now, but was it? Was she wrong? Nomi was a smart girl. But this could make a fool out of her.

The silence between them was becoming unbearable.

Nomi definitely didn't want a boyfriend. She wasn't ready for that. And she . . . well, she didn't want Arthur to ask her to the dance. Mostly. Kind of. That part was more confusing. Was it possible to want opposite things at the same time?

She was still mad at him for the way he'd ended the friendship. And she was even madder for the way he'd restarted it, as if it were so easy. And she was *maddest* about him confusing her.

Look: Annihilation was nigh, and Nomi was thinking about Arthur.

Completely illogical, that was for sure. She wished she could take all her feelings and shove them into a carefully dated box, for some future kid to discover and wonder how, with everything happening in the world, she still cared about dances and crushes.

"Then I guess we'll see each other there!" she said, too enthusiastically.

Arthur bobble-headed a yes, and she couldn't tell if he was relieved or disappointed.

They continued sorting through the old letters in silence, box after box. Then they sorted through old maps, which were pretty cool, showing how the area used to have a lot of hotels run by Japanese immigrants. But that couldn't possibly lead them to the book.

Finally, Nomi admitted the truth. "The sequel's not here."

"Yeah . . ." Arthur looked up, like he was coming up from underwater. "Right. Yeah."

She closed 1889, then set the maps back on the cart. Looking at all this history, she got that spindly-tingling feeling, that feeling that was *not* magic, not in any way, but was . . . something.

"But we *will* find it," she promised, burying her disappointment, and the weirdness, and all that awful uncertainty under that spindly-*something*. "And then we will know exactly what to do."

ARTHUR

CROSS-COUNTRY PRACTICE WAS CANCELED DUE TO the smoke, which meant Arthur had nothing to do, and that made him want to kick something. Instead, he threw a tennis ball against his bedroom wall and paced. His homework had only taken an hour, which meant he had way too much energy and way too much time to think about yesterday.

Why had he brought up the dance? Thank god Nomi had changed the subject. He wasn't *really* about to ask her to go with him—right?

His mind sprinted, replaying their conversation all through the afternoon, and then all through dinner, and he knew his dads were starting to get curious, so before they could ask, he stood abruptly. "I'll do the dishes," he offered, grabbing the dinner they'd just barely finished eating.

Chores. A peace offering, so they'd leave him in peace.

It didn't work.

As soon as he turned on the tap, his dads joined him in the kitchen.

"I'll wash, you dry," Abba said—and what choice did Arthur have? He stepped aside, letting his dad take the lead.

"Sooo . . ." Danthony dragged the word out as he hopped onto the counter. "We know there's a dance tomorrow . . ."

Arthur had known this was coming. They'd been trying to give him more space since sixth grade (*It's good for development,* Danthony had explained, *though it kills us.*), but Arthur knew they weren't gonna let his first middle-school dance pass without comment.

Abba chimed in. "And we know this is probably the age where you and your friends are talking about crushes . . ."

Arthur ran a dishrag over a pot. He wanted to crawl inside it. Anything, *anything*, to avoid talking about girls with his parents.

"Lucas thinks I'm gay," he said, and then instantly regretted it.

He didn't dare look at his dads, but he knew they were probably exchanging a loaded glance.

"Are you having feelings?" Abba asked.

Arthur *felt* like he wanted this conversation to end.

Danthony laughed. "Of course he has feelings. No need to be vague. Arthur, are you having romantic feelings for boys?"

"Oh god," Arthur said.

"You know you can tell us," Danthony insisted.

Arthur did know that. Which was nice and all. But still. He couldn't imagine a more awkward conversation.

Well, aside from yesterday's conversation . . . Why on earth had he brought up the dance?

"You know, most kids don't tell their parents about their crushes," Arthur said, as he dried a plate. "Because it's super awkward."

Another glance was exchanged before Abba asked, "Is Lucas . . . teasing you about this?"

"Oh no, Lucas doesn't care. I mean, I'm not gay, but he wouldn't care if I was," Arthur said. "He'd be cool with it."

Danthony blurted, "*Lucas* would be cool with it?"

Arthur tensed. His dads were always so cautious about Lucas. Even though they never said it, Arthur knew they didn't like him. "What's that supposed to mean?" He was basically attacking the dish.

"It's just . . ." Danthony said. "When I was younger, Lucas was the kind of kid who would've stuffed me in a locker."

Arthur turned to his dads. They were looking at one another now—more wordless communication, full of love and sympathy and emotions Arthur couldn't quite follow.

"But you kids are different, of course." Abba looked back at Arthur, his voice soft. "You give us hope."

Unexpectedly, Arthur felt something thick and hot kick inside him. His throat scratched, like he'd been running through smoke. If he was being honest, he'd tell them he didn't *want* to be a source of hope. It was too much pressure.

"He's right," Danthony said. "And no matter what, we're proud of you. No matter what, you can talk to us.

Middle school is a big, confusing time, with big, confusing feelings—"

"Thanks," Arthur interrupted, as he dried the last of the dishes. It was so clean he could see his reflection. "I've gotta go work on the social studies project."

He could tell his dads wanted to say more, but they decided not to push him. Abba nodded. "You've been spending a lot of time on that."

Arthur shrugged. "Yeah. Well, mostly Nomi is. But I'm helping." He didn't want to talk about Nomi, but he also kinda did. It felt both nice and terrible to think about her, like scratching a mosquito bite. "She's getting closer to finding the sequel."

Danthony frowned. "Sequel?"

"To that book. There's a second one." Arthur walked toward his room, but Danthony stopped him.

"Hang on."

Something in his dad's tone made him want to bolt. If Arthur could make a prophecy of his own, he'd say that whatever his dad was about to tell him wasn't something he wanted to hear.

"Come with me," Danthony said.

And though Arthur absolutely did not want to, though walking down those stairs felt like stuffing his skin into a bottle, he followed his dad into the dimly lit museum. The art seemed to buzz around them, as if it had too much energy.

Arthur watched as Danthony typed his login into the old desktop.

"We don't know *who* drops the art off." His dad pulled up a spreadsheet and scrolled back through time. "But we keep track of *what* comes in . . ."

He scrolled past a painting entry, then a set of speckled bowls, until: "Yeah, here it is. 'October fourteenth, 2021. Old leather binding, Stone and Taylor Printing Company, handwritten poetry. A set of books. Two.'"

All that bottled energy exploded, and Arthur lurched toward his dad, accidentally banging against the desk. "So you have the sequel?"

After all that searching, all Nomi's puzzling, the sequel was right there in the museum. They'd found it. *He'd* found it.

And he'd get to tell Nomi. She'd smile so big her cheeks would crease.

"No," his dad said.

Arthur frowned, unsure what his dad was responding to. "No what?"

His dad pointed to the screen, and Arthur read along. "'First book: relatively good condition. Second book: mildewing, crumbling, pages ripped. Thrown out.'"

Arthur stared. *Thrown out.* His head began to pound. "Thrown . . . out?" he repeated, like he'd forgotten how to speak.

"We try to save everything," his dad said.

Arthur couldn't move. He stared at those words so hard they wobbled.

"But if something's unsalvageable," Danthony continued, "we have to throw it out."

"Like, in the garbage?" Arthur didn't know why he was asking. It wasn't like his dad was gonna say, *Oh, no, silly! In a storage unit right over here!*

"I'm sorry," his dad said. "If I'd known you were looking for a second book I would've said something earlier. I didn't think it mattered."

Truthfully, Arthur himself had wondered if it mattered. He figured he was going along for the ride, because maybe he could be helpful. And Nomi and Vi cared. And he and Nomi . . . Nomi was . . . well, whatever, that was beside the point.

But now a feeling he couldn't name wriggled inside him.

Everyone was always talking about the terrible things that might happen, and it was like he'd been living with his breath held. He'd been waiting for the book so he could see what came next, so he could *breathe*, and now—

Briefly, he let himself consider the local dump. He grasped at a fantasy: They could go there and rescue the book.

But this was years ago. The book had been crumbling when it arrived. Surely, it had rotted away by now, dissolved back into the earth.

So that was it.

There was no sequel. No more mysterious little poems. No more guessing what they might mean for the future. No more fake group project. No more Nomi.

And that was already bad enough, but on top of everything else—Arthur was the one who had to tell her.

WE TREES KNOW WHAT IT'S LIKE WHEN THE SKY GOES dry. We know what it's like to wait for rain that doesn't come and doesn't come and doesn't come. We know drought.

During the Second World War, the boy who painted signs stopped painting signs. His government turned on him, forcing his family and his Japanese community into camps.

Drought years are long years. Painful years. In the camp, his mother would speak of the hotel they'd had to give up. What had become of it? On good nights, she'd recite her favorite dream like a fairy tale: Maybe it became an art school, like the one she'd attended when she was young.

But no. In truth, it sat empty until years after the war, when the boy, now a man, returned to the hotel. He'd saved up a nearly impossible amount, determined to become one of the few Japanese Americans to reclaim what they'd had.

His following months were frantic. He hardly slept, and after spending all his money to buy back the hotel, he had to sell most of his belongings to make ends meet.

So when a young Black woman walked by his street sale, she could tell he needed help.

The same war that had sent him away from the city had brought her there. She'd moved up from Arkansas to Washington to build planes, and though she still spent most of her days on the assembly line, her true love was history. In another life, in another world, she might've been a fancy museum curator in New York or DC, or—who knew—Paris, even.

But in this life, she could only afford the cheapest thing on his table: a pair of old journals. It was the best she could do, and anyway, when she held them, she could feel history crackling around her. She imagined she'd sell them to a New York City museum one day.

So she whisked the tree away, and it sat in her attic for many long years.

Eventually, the tree would find readers again. Eventually, seeds would grow roots.

But it would be many decades before that.

In that time, history would ring with protests and boycotts and movements. Fires would burn, some of them leaving everything charred beyond recognition, others letting new growth flourish.

But those decades were long. Those decades were thirsty.

The world waited for rain. It waited and waited as heat smoldered.

Rain would come, eventually. But we trees know: Sometimes it doesn't come soon enough.

VI

VI WAS SITTING ON NOMI'S BEDROOM FLOOR, GETTING ready for the dance in a few hours, but her mind was in her phone, pixelated and disembodied, because it had been days since she'd sent it and Lucas still hadn't opened the photo.

Snapchat told her when someone viewed her photo, and then the photo would promptly disappear, but last she'd checked (ninety seconds ago), it still sat there, waiting for Lucas, unacknowledged.

"Are you texting Lucas?" Nomi asked.

Vi jolted as she looked up from her phone. She hadn't even realized she was checking it. Again. She existed in two different times—now, and in the moment she sent the photo.

Here, now, the gray was pressing against Nomi's bedroom windows, and Nomi was watching her expectantly. "Are you and Lucas texting?" Nomi repeated.

Vi considered telling the truth. It might be a relief to let someone into this lonely loop of panic. To let someone else ask the questions. *Did he get the notification? Is he ignoring it on purpose? Was this all a joke?*

But to tell Nomi would be inviting the worst question. *Violet, what have you done? Are you stupid?*

Vi shrugged. "It doesn't matter."

Except, of course, Nomi took that to mean the exact opposite. She chewed her lip, like she was biting back hurt. "What are you talking about with him that you can't talk about with me?"

Vi swallowed. She couldn't tell Nomi about the photo, but she didn't want to lie, so she told a different truth. "I don't know. It's kinda nice to talk to someone who's half Asian. He gets it."

Nomi frowned. "I could get it too. If you told me."

Vi looked at her best friend. In the smoke-bleached light, her skin was as white as the eggshells Vi was walking on. "I know, but . . ."

In first grade, second grade, third, Vi had believed that she and Nomi were connected in a deep brain-heart way, that they barely had to speak, that they just *knew* how the other felt.

But at some point—and she didn't know exactly when—that changed. Not in some giant seismic way, but in the small ways that can be even scarier. She could tell Nomi a lot. But she couldn't tell her everything.

She checked her phone again. Nothing.

Nomi's voice dropped to a whisper. "Are you gonna dance with him tonight?"

Vi shook her head. Dancing with Lucas felt so far away from their relationship. It felt, somehow, both more and less serious. "I don't think so."

Nomi's brow furrowed, like she was puzzling out a math problem. "Why not? You both like each other."

Vi shrugged. "Yeah, but . . . there are different kinds of liking someone. There's slow-dance liking, but there are other ways too."

Vi heard herself sound so confident and knowing, but she *didn't* know, exactly. Before Nomi could respond, she asked, "What about you? Are you planning to dance?"

Nomi swallowed, her embarrassment obvious. It was one of Vi's favorite things about Nomi: She wore her secrets right on her face, as unmistakable as a dash of chili pepper. "Definitely not."

"If you say so," Vi teased.

Nomi grimaced. "What do you mean?"

"Hello?" Vi prodded. Their conversation had moved past Lucas. Vi was mostly relieved, and a tiny bit disappointed. "Arthur looks at you like . . ."

Like Nomi had the answer to a question he couldn't even name.

". . . like he likes you," Vi finished.

Nomi buried her face in a pillow as she mumbled something suspiciously close to "He almost asked me to the dance."

"He *what*?" A hundred emotions flooded Vi, each with a flavor of its own, but she focused on the boldest and brightest—the joy she felt. Because if Arthur liked Nomi, that meant he appreciated her, and Nomi deserved to be appreciated.

Nomi shot a pained glance at her bedroom door. "Quiet! But yes! At the library, while you abandoned me."

"I did not *abandon* you. You're overdramatizing." Vi had no reason to feel guilty about that. She'd really had a dentist appointment. "You told me nothing interesting happened at the library!"

"It didn't." Nomi hugged the pillow. "We didn't find anything out about the book. I'm at a dead end. But I'll figure it out."

"There are interesting things besides the book, Nomi!" Vi nudged Nomi's knee. "So, do you like him back?"

Vi wasn't surprised Arthur liked Nomi. It explained a lot of his weirdness. But she *was* surprised he'd asked Nomi about the dance. Dances were so public, and Arthur was popular, and popular boys didn't always want the world to know they liked girls like Nomi.

Vi checked her phone. Nothing.

Had she gotten this terribly wrong? Maybe Lucas didn't like her at all. Maybe he was worried she had the wrong idea—that she might try to dance with him tonight, that the world might see them together, when he preferred to keep it secret.

She swallowed. *You are what you eat,* she supposed. *Taste enough secrets, and eventually you become one.*

"I don't know." Nomi hesitated. "How are you supposed to know that you like someone?"

Vi opened her mouth to answer, but found she couldn't. It was a basic thing, the most obvious of things to know about yourself, and yet. She shook her head. "I guess . . . they make you feel sick. But in a good way, not a gross way."

Nomi frowned. "That doesn't sound right."

"I'm explaining it badly. You just kinda know." Vi didn't want to talk about this anymore. She leaned forward, like she could fall face-first into distraction. "Anyway, let me do your makeup."

Nomi made a strangled noise.

"Come on!" Vi pulled her makeup bag out of her tote. At the start of sixth grade, her mom had taken her to the makeup aisle of Bartell's. *You're a middle schooler now,* she'd declared as she'd plucked an orange tube of mascara off the shelf.

That whole anecdote had ended up on Instagram.

"I'm not a makeup girl," Nomi insisted.

Her tone reminded Vi of what her dad had said, at the dinner table. *Girl stuff.* Suddenly, this felt very important. "There's no such thing as a *makeup girl*. There're just girls who wear makeup sometimes. Because it's fun. Please? Let me do this?"

Nomi eyed the makeup bag like it might eat her.

Vi tried to smile. "Don't you wanna feel pretty when Arthur asks you to dance?"

Vi felt pretty, mostly. She'd settled on a brand-new daisy-dotted dress, which she liked because it made her feel at least two years older, even though the fabric itched.

Nomi, on the other hand, wore jeans and a T-shirt. But Vi liked that, too. Her friend didn't look older or younger. She just looked like *Nomi*.

Nomi groaned. "First of all, you can't *feel* pretty. You can feel angry, or excited, or scared, when your body triggers the fight-or-flight response. That's factual biology. But there's no *pretty* feeling."

"Nomi," Vi groaned. Surely her friend was being intentionally dense?

"Second of all!" Nomi continued. "Arthur is not going to ask me to dance. Probably."

All Vi had to do was give her friend a look. And Nomi relented.

"Fine." She tossed the pillow aside and scooted forward. "I *am* kinda curious what I'd look like. For scientific reasons."

"Of course."

"But let's make a pact." Nomi reached her pinky out. "This isn't for them. No boys tonight."

Vi almost laughed. They hadn't pinky promised since fifth grade. "And what are we gonna do if a certain boy comes over and asks you to dance?"

"If any boys come over, I will say, 'Get away, pelican brain.'"

"You absolutely would not say that. You'd get in trouble, and you hate getting in trouble."

Nomi nodded seriously. "Well, I will think it."

Now Vi really did laugh. She locked her pinky around Nomi's. Maybe it was just the cozy safety of Nomi's bedroom, but suddenly Vi felt like the outside world couldn't touch her.

"No boys," she promised. "Tonight is ours."

NOMI

THE NIGHT WAS THEIRS.

Well, kinda.

They got to the school late, because Vi had taken her time swiping eyeliner across Nomi's lids, then wiping it off (*it's easier to do it on your own face,* Vi insisted), then trying again and again until Nomi's eyes burned. Finally, Vi had stepped aside so Nomi could see herself in the mirror.

She'd blinked once, twice, as a prickling sensation rose behind her eyes.

And, okay, maybe Nomi made things into too big of a deal, and maybe this didn't have to feel so big, but—

Fact: She looked better than she ever had.

Fact: She looked almost *pretty*.

And fact: She didn't look like herself anymore.

She didn't know how to fit those truths together. If this was what pretty felt like, she wasn't sure she liked it.

"It looks . . ." She'd started to say *wrong*, but then she saw Vi's face, all hopeful and excited, and said, "Good?"

So that's how Nomi ended up standing in front of the school gym, wearing a face that was only kind of hers.

"Ready?" Vi asked.

Nomi nodded. She couldn't tell if she felt terrified or giddy. It was silly to care this much about a dance. Calamity was at stake, after all!

But as she pulled the gym doors open, her whole body fizzed.

Inside, a giant banner read: *FunDance! Let's help the Forest Service!* Above them, carved wooden ornaments of miniature trees hung like stars. On the walls, trees made out of tissue paper formed a makeshift forest, which was lit up in scattered color by flashing disco lights. On the dance floor, a DJ pumped a beat into the gym, and a fog machine piped sour candy scented smoke into the air.

Despite herself, Nomi felt herself falling in love with this night. This was what her classmates had paid so much for: the chance to be part of something *more* for a night. Something bigger than every other day.

Across the gym, her favorite teacher, Mr. Romero, spotted them and approached. "Like the decorations? The kids and I made them," he said, with undisguised pride. He was the faculty head of the student FunDance committee. "You know, everyone who gets involved with FunDance loves it. It's always nice to get creative, and do some good for the world at the same time."

This was why he was Nomi's favorite—not only because

she loved math, but because he was just so excited about everything he said.

"There's still one more year for you two to try it," he added.

Vi nodded and said, in her polite-to-teachers voice, "We'll think about it."

Mr. Romero smiled. "Well, have fun tonight," he said, and then he left them, to have fun, presumably.

A few kids were dancing, but most were clumped up around the snack tables.

"Should we dance?" Nomi asked.

"Nobody else is really . . ." Vi looked up from her phone—but not to look at Nomi. She was scanning the gym, and Nomi knew she was looking for Lucas.

He wasn't there yet, and neither was Arthur (not that Nomi had noticed), and as Vi turned back to her phone, frustration flared in Nomi's chest.

It was fine, really, totally and completely fine that Vi had changed her name and her clothes and was *talking-talking* to Lucas.

It was fine that Vi wanted privacy, even though best friends didn't *need* privacy. It was fine.

But did Vi have to do that *now*? It was like Nomi's "No Boys" pact hadn't mattered, her words hadn't mattered, she—

She wanted to dance. The DJ started playing "Dancing Queen," and it felt almost like a dare.

"Come on." Nomi nudged Vi, sounding as desperate as she felt. "The night is ours, right?"

Vi slid her phone back into her pocket, and Nomi almost asked what Vi was so worried about, but instead she grabbed Vi's hands and tugged her onto the mostly empty dance floor.

"What are you doing?" Vi protested, but she was laughing a little.

The only other kids dancing were even less cool than Nomi, not that Nomi cared, because she very proudly didn't even *notice* those things, and she shouted to Vi over the music, "Don't fight it!"

"Don't fight what—" Vi started, but then Nomi began to spin, keeping their hands clasped together. They were moving so fast, anchored only by each other. If they let go, they would fall.

"How are we gonna stop?" Vi asked.

"Who cares?" They'd have to stop eventually. Nomi was getting dizzy. But . . . who cared indeed? That was a problem for the future, and for once she had no plan. Lucas and Arthur would get there soon, and Vi was on the edge of *possibility*, and Nomi might turn to flame, and nothing would ever be the same, but right now they were spinning.

Color danced around them, and in the sweet-sour smoke, Nomi almost forgot about the real smoke outside, about the book that told the future, about Arthur and all that strangeness. Maybe, possibly, the night really could be theirs—

And then her hands slipped, and the two of them went flying backward—laws of inertia and gravity and all that—before landing on their butts.

A flash of pain lit Nomi's tailbone. But Vi laughed with a slightly wild edge in her eyes, so Nomi stood and laughed too, rubbing the pain away.

Look, Vi mouthed, nodding over Nomi's shoulder.

More kids were dancing now, lured to the floor by the song's promise of *having the time of their lives.* And then, at the edge of the crowd, Nomi spotted Arthur.

Her stomach rolled as the future caught up with her.

"Dancing Queen" ended. A slow song began to play.

Arthur walked closer. And closer.

Fact: Nomi's hands started to shake, a side effect of her triggered sympathetic nervous system, which she'd learned about in science—

"Oh," Vi murmured. At first Nomi thought Vi was responding to Arthur, but when she looked over, Vi was staring at her phone, the color draining from her face.

"What?" Nomi asked.

But Vi shook her head. "Nothing," she said. "Have fun with Arthur."

"Wait—" Nomi protested, but Vi was already stepping back, to the edge of the crowd, and there was Arthur, right in front of her.

Around them, couples began to form. Nomi wanted to vanish.

"Nomi." Arthur ran a hand through his hair and started

speaking quickly, a string of words she couldn't make out over the music.

"What?" she shouted.

He repeated himself, looking rather pained.

She repeated herself, also pained. "WHAT?"

He leaned in closer. He smelled like body spray, which wasn't *bad*, but wasn't exactly good. "I have to talk to you."

He was going to ask her to dance. Fact.

She wanted him to. Also fact.

He did that open-and-close thing with his mouth like he couldn't figure out how to speak, which made sense, because Nomi felt the same way.

But she'd learned a thing or two from her mother's feminist lessons.

She took a deep breath, and they spoke at the same time.

"Do you want to dance?" she asked.

"My dad threw the book away," he said. And then: "Oh, uh, yeah, I guess, sure."

Nomi blinked. The song sounded miles away, like the world had gone on mute. "What did you say?" she asked. Only this time she'd heard him; she just didn't want to. She felt her insides going gray.

He squirmed, his face going pink. "The sequel. I didn't know until yesterday. It was moldy or something, I don't know, and . . ."

He kept talking, but Nomi stopped listening. Three facts to note:

He didn't like her, actually.

His dad threw the book away. And . . .

The world was blurring around her, like she'd never stopped spinning.

"We have to go to the dump," she said. "Right now."

Arthur shook his head. "He threw it away years ago. There's no book, Nomi. Not anymore."

"But . . ." Nomi stumbled for the right words. "That's not possible."

Of course there was still a book. It wasn't like it had just turned to ash. It was out there, it had always been out there, and they just had to find it, they had to persist, because that was how this worked, how it *had* to work—

Arthur looked at the floor, like he'd dropped something heavy. "I'm sorry."

"I don't . . ." But Nomi didn't have time to find the words, because Lucas, Gregory, and a few more of Arthur's terrible friends came up behind him, jostling him in that aggressive boy way.

Startled, Arthur took two huge steps away from Nomi, like she was terminally uncool and it was contagious.

She tried not to feel hurt. What did Arthur's reaction matter when there was no hope for the future?

"Lucas needs to show you something," Gregory said to Arthur, speaking way too loudly, as usual.

Arthur turned away from her, but Nomi could still see the side of his face, flaming red, even in the blue and green disco lights. She wondered if she should leave, but then again, she'd been here first. Arthur was the one who'd slunk up and ruined her whole night.

"Show me what?" Arthur asked.

Lucas just laughed—and call it observation, call it probability, call it a *feeling*—whatever it was, Nomi knew. This was it, the final prophecy coming true. This was annihilation. Calamity.

The boys dragged Arthur away and out of the gym, leaving Nomi alone, and she turned, looking for her friend.

But Vi was gone.

ARTHUR

"ALL RIGHT, BOYS, GATHER ROUND," LUCAS ANNOUNCED. He'd brought them to the boys' locker room, which was dark except for a single flickering light, quiet except for them. "Someone give me a drumroll."

Alfie beat his hands against one of the benches, *bumbumbum*, in sync with Arthur's pounding heart. It sounded a little threatening,

Lucas pulled out his phone and grinned. In the dim light, he looked a little threatening, too. "Vi sent me a picture."

Arthur understood instantly. He closed his eyes, trying to will himself into the past, back to ten minutes ago when his biggest problem was a missing book of poetry.

"Violet Kim," Gregory snorted. "No way. How'd you get that out of Quiet Violet?"

"Guess she trusted me," Lucas said, shooting Gregory a look. "You aren't the only one."

Arthur didn't know what that meant, but whatever. The

weird competition between those two felt particularly stupid at that moment.

He tried not to think about the question Vi had asked him. *Do you trust Lucas?*

Of course, he'd replied. *He's my guy.*

His legs burned in the way they did when he needed to run. He needed to run. He hadn't in too long—this smoke had ruined everything.

Lucas started showing the picture to the guys, who started reacting. A small part of Arthur was curious, which he hated. Even thinking about it was a betrayal of Vi, and a betrayal of Nomi, and for a second his anger flamed so blinding bright he couldn't see.

He hadn't asked for this, but here was yet another log thrown onto the towering pile of guilt that didn't, or shouldn't, or couldn't belong to him.

The ground he walked on was stolen. And all guys were terrible. And the forest was on fire.

What was he supposed to do with all this kindling?

Gregory gripped his shoulder. "Aw, look, Arthur's blushing. So innocent."

"No—" Arthur said.

Lucas laughed. "Nah, he's just not into girls."

"No—that's not—I'm not—" Arthur sputtered. He ran a hand through his hair. He needed to get out of there.

"You can tell us the truth," Lucas insisted.

"That is the truth."

All the boys stared at him, disbelieving, smirking. Maybe his friends wouldn't be *completely* cool if they thought he was gay. Maybe the rules were more complicated than he'd thought.

Lucas held his phone carelessly. If Arthur leaned over, he could see what was on it. He could react like everyone else. He could push all this squirmy attention off himself and put it right back onto Vi.

He swallowed. All guys were terrible, right? He was born into it. What choice did he have?

"Prove it," Gregory said.

Arthur hesitated. "I . . ."

"He's scared," Alfie goaded, and the other guys laughed, even though Arthur was absolutely positive that Alfie was terrified.

Arthur hadn't been scared, but whatever, now he kinda was. Now he wondered about their principal, and their parents, and getting expelled. "I thought we're supposed to be careful," he blurted.

Lucas stared at him.

"Because," Arthur explained, feeling silly, "it's hard to be a guy."

"Oh yeah," Lucas said. "But that's about, like, what you're allowed to say."

The fire built in Arthur's legs, arms, his whole body.

Lucas held the phone out. All Arthur wanted to do was run.

NOMI

NOMI RAN THROUGH THE BATHROOM DOOR.

"VI! ARE YOU IN HERE?" Her ears were ringing, and she knew she was shouting because the three girls by the sinks raised their brows.

One of them pointed to a closed stall. "Violet Kim? She's in there. I think she's upset."

Nomi rushed over, ready to unload the earth-shattering book news at top speed—there'd be no help, no guidance, no way to survive the total annihilation of flame—but a soft sniffling from behind the door stopped her.

Vi was crying. Had she already heard about the book? But it couldn't be that, because she'd been gone by the time Arthur told Nomi.

"Boy drama?" one of the girls whispered.

Nomi opened her mouth to respond, then realized she didn't know.

"Boys are the worst," another added with an eye roll.

The girls exchanged a glance, then gave Nomi genuinely

sympathetic looks before flitting out of the bathroom, gossiping about their own lives, laughing to themselves because their worlds weren't falling apart.

Nomi wanted to bang on the door, burst it open, demand that Vi tell her what was wrong so she could devise a plan to fix it.

But she stopped herself. This wasn't the moment for Level 5 Nomi. What would Vi do?

She swallowed, raised her hand, and knocked—gently. "It's me," she said.

Slowly, the stall door creaked open, and Nomi found her friend sitting on the dirty tile floor. She'd wrapped her arms so tightly around her knees that she looked smaller than a twelve-year-old should. When she looked up at Nomi, her eyes were red.

"He screenshotted it," she croaked.

Nomi shook her head, uncomprehending.

So Vi told her everything: about her mom's Instagram, about trusting Lucas, about a picture that was both her and not her.

And Nomi stood, paralyzed, because all she could do was listen.

"I'm sorry," Vi whispered, though Nomi had no idea why she was apologizing. "I'm not the person you think I should be. I'm so stupid."

"You aren't stupid," Nomi insisted, a little more harshly than she meant to. *Not the person you think I should be?* What was that supposed to mean?

When Vi flinched, Nomi repeated, softer, "You aren't stupid."

Last week, if Vi had told Nomi what she was planning to do, would Nomi have called it stupid? Nomi didn't know. She'd heard about this stuff happening, to other girls, in other schools. And what had Nomi thought of them? She'd never been able to understand it, to fit herself into someone else's mind and see why they made their choices. But what happened when that someone else was Vi, her best friend, the person whose mind she knew best in the world?

She couldn't think straight. All she knew was that her hands were shaking, on account of her nervous system, et cetera. All this had been happening to Vi, and Nomi hadn't known, and now Vi was sitting on a dirty bathroom floor, and Nomi hadn't been there, but now here she was.

Annihilation.

She felt physically ill with rage, but she tried to arrange her thoughts into a straight line, tried to soothe herself with facts.

Fact: Vi was still her best friend in the world.

Fact: Lucas had hurt her best friend in the world.

And fact: Nomi was going to burn him to the ground.

THERE'S A STORY HUMANS TELL. YOU MIGHT HAVE heard it. A bedtime story, a book about a tree that gives, and a human who takes.

PART IV

✦

A girl who burns, a boy who breaks.

VI

LUCAS HAD CARED ABOUT HER. VI KNEW THAT. BUT knowing that didn't make it better. It was worse, really, because caring about her hadn't mattered in the end. It was like, no matter how much he cared, how much they'd truly connected, some invisible hand had come along and pushed him into hurting her.

Or maybe that was giving him too much credit. Maybe he hadn't cared at all. Maybe there was no invisible hand—just his. Vi didn't know how to make sense of it, and her thoughts circled and circled until her heart felt trapped and small.

He hadn't even responded. He'd just screenshotted her photo without a word, as if that was all he'd wanted in the first place.

Nomi had invited her to sleep over, but all Vi wanted was to be alone. She didn't want anyone looking at her ever again.

She pulled her blankets over her head, searching for some kind of safety, but it was useless. She'd been alone in her room when this started, and now look. Even with her phone off and shoved in her dresser, she felt raw, like the entire world could see her.

With a knock, the door creaked open. "Honey?" her mom said. "Do you want to talk about whatever happened?"

From beneath the covers, Vi shook her head. But her mom walked in, and the mattress shifted as she sat down.

Vi felt her mom's hand on her shoulder. "Whoever he is, he isn't worth it," she promised.

Vi chewed the inside of her cheek until she tasted blood, because that was exactly the problem. If he wasn't worth it, then all of this was for nothing.

"This isn't about a boy," Vi lied.

Her mom hesitated. "Oh, Violet, I shouldn't have assumed. You know you can tell me anything."

"I can't," Vi blurted. "Because you'll tell everyone."

"Violet? I don't—"

"I found your Instagram."

"My . . ." Her mom sounded lost. "This is about my Instagram?"

"Your *Raising Wildflowers* account." Vi hadn't realized how angry she was until she heard it in her voice. "Raising me and Blue. You post about *us*."

"I don't understand." Her mom's voice was annoyingly gentle. "Did the kids at school find it? Did something happen?"

"No, *I* found it." Vi's breath was hot under the blanket.

She didn't understand why her mom didn't understand. "So you're an *influencer* now?"

She spat the word like it tasted rotten. *Influencer.*

"Honey . . . I wasn't trying to be—this wasn't to . . ." Her mom pulled her hand away, and the empty space it left on Vi's arm grew cold. "It's hard to explain, but when you become a mom, sometimes you disappear. It's like the person I was before just stopped existing. And it wasn't your fault or Blue's, not at all. You two are perfect. But it was everyone else. No one *saw* me anymore."

And too many people saw Vi. She was starting to sweat under the covers, but she didn't want to face her mom.

"Then I started the blog," her mom continued, "because I was so lonely, and I didn't think anyone would read it, but they did. Everything just kind of grew from there, and suddenly I could tell my story again."

A part of Vi felt bad for her mom. But when she closed her eyes, she could see those photos, those captions, those comments. *Is it silly to feel like I know her?*

"But you didn't tell your story," she bit out. "You told mine."

Vi couldn't see her mom, but she felt the words fill the room, choking. She waited for her mom's response. And waited.

The bed shifted again as her mother stood up. Very softly, she said, "You are my story." And then: "I'm really sorry, Vi."

The footsteps retreated. The door clicked shut. And finally Vi threw off her covers.

As angry as she was, she wanted to call for her mom to come back, to sit there again, to see Vi.

But instead Vi was alone in her too-white room, beneath her too-childish canopy, with her too-loud thoughts.

The Instagram account wasn't the whole problem, of course. The problem was all of it, all of her, her and not her.

She didn't want to think about what Lucas had done with the picture, but she knew how this went. He'd almost certainly shown it to all his friends by now.

Her mom had been handing out Vi's secrets, piece by piece, for years. But Lucas had shared her biggest one. That secret belonged to everyone now, and it tasted like nothing.

Which was fitting. It was silly, really, to believe her private life had any flavor at all.

ARTHUR

HE HADN'T SEEN ANYTHING.

He hadn't looked at the picture, which was good, but a part of him had wanted to, and that was the part he couldn't forgive.

His feet pounded against the indoor track. Cross-country practice was going fine, better than he'd expected, which was weird, because he'd expected things to be strained between him and his teammates.

And yet they treated him normally. If there was any weirdness, it was coming from him. Vi had skipped school that day, and he couldn't stop worrying about that.

He ran harder, so hard his stomach churned. He was pushing himself too much, too early, and he knew it.

It would have been better if they could run through an actual park, but here they were, on this awful indoor track, going in circles and circles.

There was so much smoke outside and they were all supposed to ignore it. How were you supposed to live in a world on fire?

He passed the finish line, which was also the starting line, again.

Lucas was up ahead, and Arthur could lap him if he tried, so he pushed his muscles, and his stomach swirled. Suddenly this felt important, like a test Arthur had to pass. He was gaining, and distantly he heard his coach tell him to slow down, but he had momentum now, why waste it? He was so close—

Their coach blew the whistle, telling them to stop, and Arthur doubled over, hands on knees, gasping for air.

"Dude," someone said.

But Arthur didn't look up. His legs wobbled. His lungs burned. He couldn't breathe. And it wasn't enough. There was still so much *something* in him, all of it, with nowhere to go.

NOMI

NOMI DIDN'T KNOW WHERE TO GO. VI HAD FAKED SICK yesterday, which Nomi understood, but when Vi still wasn't at the tree on Tuesday morning, Nomi began to panic. They'd texted a bit, but Nomi hadn't seen Vi since the dance. Was that a mistake? Should she abandon school and find her way to Vi's house right that second? Or would *that* be the mistake?

She ended up waiting by Vi's locker, and when Vi finally arrived, just minutes before the first bell, Nomi's relief only lasted for seconds. Dark circles rimmed Vi's eyes. She left her cloth mask on, shielding her lungs from the smoke and her face from the world. She'd traded her pink for jeans and a gray hoodie pulled up over her head.

Nomi had spent so much time stressing about the pink clothes. Now she'd do anything to have them back. "You okay?" she asked.

Vi's voice was a flat line. "Doesn't matter."

"Of course it does!"

In the hallway, a couple of boys looked over, and Nomi tried to gauge what that meant. Did they know? Did *everyone* know? She hated not knowing.

The past few days, Vi's social media had been smattered with comments from anonymous accounts, and even some from kids using their real names—all flame emojis. Mocking her. *She's hot.*

"I deleted all the comments," Nomi said. Vi had given Nomi her password so Nomi could extinguish every flame without worrying Vi.

"Thanks," Vi said, sounding tired but also grateful, or at least Nomi hoped.

Then Vi opened her locker, and two scraps of paper floated to the floor. She reached down to pick them up, then stared at them, hiding the contents from Nomi.

"What's that?" Nomi asked.

"Nothing." Vi shoved them back into her locker.

But Nomi placed a hand on her wrist. "Please?"

Vi hesitated, and Nomi didn't think she could stand all this distance. "Please," she repeated. "Let me see."

Slowly, Vi handed them over, and when Nomi saw them, it was all she could do not to rip them to pieces. Crude stick-figure drawings of a girl, naked, with big boobs. "I'm gonna kill him," she said.

"You don't know who drew these," Vi mumbled.

Nomi opened her mouth to protest, because why was Vi trying to *defend him*? But then she stopped. Because she was right. It wasn't *just* Lucas.

Lucas has something to show you, Gregory had said when he'd pulled Arthur away.

Nomi had been so consumed with rage for Lucas that she hadn't even thought about Arthur. But he'd been there as well, and he just *went along with it?*

She was gonna kill him, too.

The bell rang. She and Vi would have to separate.

"We could skip class," Nomi suggested. "Sit under the tree."

Vi raised a brow, because they both knew it was an empty offer. Nomi would get in trouble. Her scholarship could get revoked.

"I'll be fine," Vi insisted.

Which was nice in theory, but Nomi wasn't so sure. She watched as Vi crumpled those drawings and stuffed them into her backpack. "I'm fine," she repeated.

The second bell rang, and Nomi walked away from Vi, her legs feeling heavy, her lungs feeling raw.

NOMI

SHE SHOULD HAVE CUT CLASS. THAT WAS ALL NOMI could think during science, during English, and especially during honors math, because even though she loved it, she shared that class with Lucas.

He was sitting at the other end of the room with Alfie, acting like everything was totally fine and normal, while she wished she could be anywhere else.

Did kids even cut class in real life? She wasn't sure. *She* certainly didn't. But she might now, because who knew, the world didn't work the way she thought.

They were solving for x today, which was ridiculous because Nomi couldn't solve for a single thing in her life.

"Nomi?" Mr. Romero asked.

Nomi looked up and realized he'd been calling on her for an answer. What was the question? For the first time, she hadn't done the homework.

"Um," she said.

The whole class turned toward her, and the feeling of their eyes was suffocating. How many of the boys knew about Vi's picture? Lucas, obviously. Alfie, for sure. But more? Had they sent it around?

"Do you have an answer?" Mr. Romero prodded.

Nomi waited for the flood of embarrassment, for the horror—because she always had an answer. But it didn't come. "No," she said.

His eyes softened. "That's okay."

She waited for the whispers—*Nomi Hastings doesn't know!*—but those didn't come either. Her classmates just looked down at their own papers, hoping they wouldn't be called on next.

Lucas raised his hand. "I do."

Mr. Romero turned to him expectantly, but as Lucas opened his mouth, Nomi interrupted.

"No," she repeated.

Mr. Romero frowned. "It's okay, Nomi. Lucas can take this one."

But *no*, because Lucas took everything. Vi had trusted him, more than she'd trusted *Nomi*, even. Vi had told him things she hadn't felt like she could tell Nomi. Which were what, exactly? Because she could have told Nomi anything.

Vi's words echoed in her head. *I'm not the person you think I should be.*

But *Lucas* was the one who wanted Vi to be a certain way. Not Nomi.

Now, he was looking at her like she was stupid, which filled her with absolute loathing.

"*No,*" she repeated.

Mr. Romero glanced at the clock. "Okay . . . we're a couple minutes until the end of class anyway. Why don't we call it a day. Nomi, would you mind staying back?"

Yes, Nomi minded very much, but she never talked back to teachers, so she just nodded.

Around her, the whispers really did start, kids murmuring as they gathered notebooks and shouldered backpacks. Lucas nudged Alfie as they stood and said, under his breath but loud enough for Nomi to hear, "Know-It-All Nomi is losing it."

"What is *wrong* with you?" Nomi stood, her chair clattering backward, clanging to the floor.

"Whoa," Alfie laughed. "Chill."

But Nomi didn't even bother with Alfie. She stared at Lucas, and she felt so mad it hurt.

"You. Are. Such. A." She had so many words for him. She was burning with all the terrible things she wanted to say. But what came out was "PELICAN BRAIN."

For a second, the entire class was silent.

And then Lucas started to laugh—the *nerve*—like her words were worthless.

"Nomi," Mr. Romero said gently as he walked over.

But Nomi couldn't hear him, because she was too busy lunging forward, tackling Lucas to the ground.

VI

VI PULLED HER LOCKER OPEN BEFORE LUNCH TO FIND more of them, those scraps of paper ruined with stick figures. Basic, toddler-level drawings of a person scratched together with wobbling lines. The flip of hair to match her own. With the mocking kissy-lips. And of course, with the boobs, way too big to be hers, and yet she had no doubt this was meant to be her.

She had the oddest sensation of being stretched, flattened into line and then smashed into paper, two-dimensional—and she almost laughed. It was absurd. Unreal. Like this was happening to some other girl, because how could it possibly be happening to her? It was silly, right? Almost funny, right? The edges of her world smoked out, blurry, not really there—

"Hey." A voice behind her startled her, and she dropped the papers. They scattered, littering the floor, and in a snap it all felt real again.

"Sorry!" Arthur stood behind her, blood draining from his face as looked down and saw the drawings.

He crouched without hesitating, scooping them and handing them back to her. She wanted to scream, wanted to throw them in his face and shout for anyone who'd listen, THESE ARE NOT MINE.

But she took them. Pushed them into her backpack, all the way to the bottom.

"I didn't see it," Arthur mumbled. "I didn't look at the . . . you know."

She did know, and in the slope of his frown and the hollowness of his eyes, she knew he was telling the truth. She started to speak, a thank-you waiting on her tongue, but stopped. Was she really supposed to thank him? Wasn't *not looking* just common decency, a baseline no one seemed to have?

She nodded.

"And I'm not really talking to the other guys right now," he added.

Vi nodded again, and though she still couldn't bring herself to thank him, their eyes locked, and something like understanding passed between them.

If he wasn't talking to the other guys, that meant he was alone, without her and Nomi, and without his teammates.

"Um." Arthur's ears flushed. "I know you already have a lot going on, but . . . do you know if Nomi's okay?"

"Nomi?" Vi shook her head. Nomi didn't have anything

to do with this. *Vi* was the one scrawled in stick figure across those notes.

"She got in a fight with Lucas," Arthur explained, desperation creeping into his voice. "She's in the principal's office. Some of the kids that saw it happen, they said she's gonna be expelled."

IN 1982, A BOY AND A GIRL SAT UNDER A TREE. HE WAS A scholarship student at a private school, and she took a long bus ride to the public school nearby, and though they both excelled, neither could fight the feeling that their schools didn't want them.

Sometimes the boy felt like the only thing his teachers could see was his anger, and none of them could see that his anger had a source—because who could live in a world full of injustice and not feel any of it?

As for the girl, sometimes she felt like nobody could see her at all.

The only place they belonged was outside, under trees.

Beneath orange-tipped leaves, the boy did his math homework, and the girl flipped through a pair of old journals she'd found in her great-aunt's attic. That poet of a tree, which was now a book, had finally found another place to grow. (They always do.)

What do you think this means? she asked. "When canopies burn"?

It doesn't mean anything, he answered, barely glancing over. *It's just bad poetry.*

The girl's roots dug back to West Africa, to the desert date and the Boscia and the baobab. The boy's to Cebu cinnamon and Ipot palm on his Filipino dad's side, and on his mom's: here. To the peoples who lived on this spot for hundreds of years, to these Pacific Northwest trees—to cedar, to alder, to Garry oak—to us.

Do you think it's possible to make a canopy that won't burn? she asked.

All trees burn, the boy said. *Some just burn faster than others.*

The girl looked at her hands, decorated with the shadow of our leaves. She couldn't know the future, couldn't see the rings ahead: where she'd become a professor, where she'd study our roots and our memories. But she could feel . . . something.

She always sat under this particular tree because of the phrase, *I was here,* carved into the bark. The words looked old, like they'd always been there, as old as time itself. She didn't know who wrote them, and she never would, and it didn't matter.

What mattered was that the words were there, and they made her feel like time was speaking directly to her.

And anyway, the boy continued, *those journals were probably written by some random colonizer.*

That's not what these books feel like, she said. *They feel bigger than one person . . . it's hard to explain.*

If she'd asked us, we would've told her, *It's the forest, not the tree. It's the canopy. It's the roots. It's all of us that make a whole.*

But she couldn't hear us. Not yet.

Here, take them. She handed him the books, as if they could make him understand.

Because he never said no to her, he took them, and the pages whispered their memories. But he didn't listen. Not yet.

VI

VI FOUND NOMI ON THE BENCH OUTSIDE PRINCIPAL Vaughn's office, leg bouncing at the speed of sound, thumbnail clamped between her teeth.

"I heard what happened," Vi said. Their principal's office was in the admin building, tucked away across from the track and the sports fields. Kids didn't usually hang there, so the hallway outside his office was blessedly empty.

Nomi frowned. "What are you doing here?"

Vi sat down on the bench beside Nomi. She knew the bench was hard and cold, but she couldn't feel it. "I'm not leaving you alone," she said.

Nomi looked like she was going to cry, but Vi watched her swallow her feelings.

This was *Nomi*, Nomi who wore her emotions as visibly as Vi wore mascara—but her face was a mask now.

"I didn't mean to make you feel like you had to be a certain way," Nomi said. "I shouldn't have made a big deal about your name, or your clothes. I thought those changes were annihilation, but annihilation was"—she waved her hands—"everything else."

"I know." Vi knew Nomi meant well. Everything was just so jumbled.

Nomi glanced at the closed office door. "Do you want me to tell Vaughn about Lucas?"

Vi ran her palms along the bench, trying to feel the wood. The fact that the boys at school knew about the picture was terrible. But her *teachers* knowing—that was a whole other level. She shook her head, then hesitated. "If it means you won't get in trouble . . ."

"I'm not asking for me," Nomi said. "I'm asking because Lucas deserves to be punished. All those guys deserve to be punished."

Vi closed her eyes. Would that matter? She could only imagine feeling better if all this disappeared. If the past few weeks went up in smoke. "You can tell him," she said. "I'm fine."

Nomi looked at her, a real look, a best-friend look. "You're lying."

Best friends didn't always know—but when they did, it was like warmth in winter.

Nomi leaned forward, determined in that Nomi way. "I won't tell," she promised.

Surely, she understood the consequences of not telling. She'd be in much more trouble. But Vi knew from the look in her eyes that nothing was going to change her mind.

All Vi could do was whisper her thanks, because how could she ever deserve a friend like Nomi?

NOMI

NOMI WASN'T GOING TO TELL PRINCIPAL VAUGHN ABOUT Vi's photo. Of course. *Obviously.* But as she entered his office, she wasn't sure what she was going to say.

She wasn't a kid who got in trouble. Being liked by teachers was a fundamental part of what made Nomi *Nomi*. The only time she ever interacted with the principal was when he told her what a bright shining star she was.

Now, he was looking at her like she was someone different.

She crossed the threshold into his office, and his eyes fell on Vi, trailing behind her. "You can stay outside, Violet. I need to talk to Nomi."

"No," Vi said. "I mean, please. Let me be here."

Principal Vaughn seemed lost for words, but he didn't protest as Vi stepped past him and joined Nomi in the small office. As the girls took their seats, the diplomas and awards lining the wall seemed to judge them. The glass-cased trophies seemed to laugh. Nomi forced her leg to stop bouncing.

He sat down across from them and ran a hand over his cropped beard, dark against his pale skin. "Would you like to tell me what happened?"

Yes! Yes, Nomi really, really would! But Vi . . .

"Lucas was . . ." Nomi floundered. "Harassing me."

Vaughn frowned. "That's a strong word, Nomi. Mr. Romero told me Lucas was trying to answer a math question. So, would you like to try that explanation again?"

Nomi tried to breathe. That same anger flared back up in her, and she tried to stomp down on it.

Her leg started to bounce again.

"Nomi," Principal Vaughn prompted.

"It's not her fault," Vi chimed in.

But he held up a hand. "I'd like to hear from Nomi first."

"Lucas . . . he . . ." Nomi swallowed. "He's always doing stuff."

Their principal stared at her, and she was aware of how useless she sounded. She was Nomi! Nomi of the factual evidence! And this was all she could say.

"He's bad," she said. "To girls. And in general."

He nodded slowly, like he was trying to understand. "I hear that. And that's not acceptable at Pineview Academy. But violence is never the appropriate response."

"Right. But." That sounded so reasonable, the way he said it. Nomi hadn't reacted the *right* way—that was clearly true. But how was she supposed to react? What *was* the "appropriate response"? What Lucas did to Vi wasn't technically violence, but it *felt* like it.

"She was protecting me," Vi said softly.

Nomi nodded.

Their principal looked back and forth between them, and his brows drew closer together, as if he'd finally found something to care about. "From what?"

"Um." The full truth would matter. It *had* to matter. But Nomi would never betray Vi, so she searched, wildly, for a truth she could say. "They're cyberbullying her!"

They'd had a whole assembly about cyberbullying last year, so Vaughn had to care about that.

He folded his hands, setting them on the desk in front of him. "We take that very seriously here," he said, and something about his tone made Nomi want to scream. But this was good, she reminded herself. He was listening. "Can you show me the comments?"

"I—well—they—" Nomi's limbs went hot. Her vision blurry. She wondered if she was going to faint. Or die. But no—just cry, apparently. Her eyes watered, because there was no proof. Because—"I deleted them."

Vaughn cleared his throat, his discomfort obvious.

The girls at school had an ongoing joke, that he couldn't deal when they cried.

"Oh . . . You know. It's fine," he held up both hands, a panicked gesture which was maybe meant to be reassuring, but which really just said *stay away*. "You don't have to tell me. I believe there were comments. But that doesn't—"

"They're sending fire emojis," Vi told him.

"Oh. As far as I'm aware, that emoji's supposed to be . . .

a compliment?" As soon as he said it, he closed his eyes and pinched the bridge of his nose, like he really wished he hadn't spoken.

"It's not," Vi murmured.

"You're absolutely right," he nodded. "And we'll discuss appropriate social-media use in our next assembly. But for now the issue at hand is your behavior in class, Nomi."

What would become of her future? No Lamarr STEM. No University of Washington. No job. No house. No plan.

"No matter what, you must use your words."

"Well, I *tried* that," Nomi blurted, and she didn't even bother regretting it, because she was probably getting expelled anyway.

"Yes." He cleared his throat. "Mr. Romero told me you called Lucas Hill a . . . pelican brain."

"You *did*?" An almost-laugh escaped Vi's lips before she clapped a hand over her mouth.

Their principal was not laughing. "She did."

Nomi couldn't take it anymore. Might as well get to the point. "Am I getting expelled?"

Principal Vaughn hesitated before responding. "No . . ."

The tightness in Nomi's chest loosened. This was going to be okay. *She* was going to be okay. Yes, Lamarr STEM! Yes, University of Washington! Yes, future!

"You're a good student," he continued, "and this is an uncharacteristic incident. But you *are* getting suspended."

Vi shot forward. "No."

Principal Vaughn took a deep breath. "And your scholarship is being revoked."

Just as quickly as it had come, all Nomi's hope vanished. Because without her scholarship, she may as well have been expelled. Her mom could never afford tuition.

Clearly she'd learned nothing at all, because she wanted to tackle Lucas all over again. This was all his—

"It's my fault," Vi burst out.

"Wait." Nomi interrupted. "Vi—"

But Vi shook her head, and she didn't look at Nomi as she said, "I sent a picture."

HOW DO YOU HEAR THE TREES?

Take the world at a slant, ear to the ground, feel the Earth. Breathe.

Sometimes we're loud, our leaves roaring in the wind.

But often, we're quiet. Softer than a hummingbird's heartbeat. A whisper of chill in the air, the sound of temperature dropping—the moment when the sky holds its breath, the whole world waiting on the promise of rain.

VI

THE MOMENT BEFORE VI TOLD PRINCIPAL VAUGHN THE truth, her whole world went quiet.

She heard him revoke Nomi's scholarship, and then she heard nothing except the sound of her breath and her blood rushing in her ears, roaring with the knowledge that she had to say something.

She hadn't looked at Principal Vaughn when she told him what happened.

In a bra, she'd told the coffee-stained carpet beneath his desk.

Somehow, that was worse than finding out Lucas had screenshotted the photo. Worse than the stick figures. Worse than the flame emojis. Telling Principal Vaughn was worse because it made Vi feel so young and stupid. Like a little girl with no ability to live in the world.

"I see" was all Vaughn said in response.

And all Vi could do was nod.

He'd told them he had to phone their parents and call

Lucas in to talk, and now they were sitting outside his office on that hard bench, counting seconds.

Vi hated Vaughn for that. If he was gonna make her sit there, waiting for Lucas to walk past, then he clearly didn't *see* at all.

"You didn't have to do that," Nomi insisted, back to bouncy-jittery on the bench.

"Yes I did," Vi responded. She still felt numb.

Seconds tick-tick-ticked, and when footsteps sounded in the hallway, Vi looked up to see Lucas.

His don't-care hair was messier than usual, in a way that said he cared, maybe a little, and as he passed, Vi willed him to say something, to even just *look* at her. But he didn't glance in their direction before stepping into Vaughn's office. She may as well have been a ghost.

"Vaughn has to expell him," Nomi whispered, once the heavy door clicked shut. "He *has* to."

"Maybe."

Vi's mom would be there any minute now, and dread coiled around Vi's chest. Would this end up on Instagram? *My little flower is a huge disappointment.*

"Definitely!" Nomi hissed. "What Lucas did was so wrong. And illegal, probably!"

Vi swallowed, pulling her thoughts back to Nomi. "At the very least, Vaughn should change his mind about your scholarship," she said. "You were just defending me."

"You think he would?" Nomi asked, legs shaking, fingers

tapping, bubbling like shaken soda. "Maybe I could write a letter. An *essay*. Teachers love essays."

The building door banged open and Vi looked up, expecting to see her mom, but she found Lucas's dad instead. Before she could snap her gaze back to the swirling floor, his eyes captured hers. They were unfeeling, dense, as suffocating as the smoke outside—they made Vi want to crawl out of her skin. Lucas had texted, once: **My dad's too much.**

She hadn't thought to ask, *Too much of what?*

He opened Principal Vaughn's door without asking for permission, and then slammed it behind him, so loud Vi's teeth hurt.

Nomi glared at the closed door. "Well, I guess that's where Lucas gets it."

"Lucas isn't as bad as his dad," Vi said, and then hated herself for defending him.

Nomi inhaled like there was a whole lot she wanted to say, but she sighed it all out. "That's a low bar."

They didn't have to wait long for their own parents. Vi's mom rushed in—straight from Pilates, looking like a movie mom in her matching leggings and tank top—followed by Nomi's, who was still wearing her grocery-store name tag, and was spewing a string of curse words.

"What on Earth?" Nomi's mom asked, once she'd finished swearing.

So they told their moms everything. The photo. Math class. Pelican brain. Suspension. Scholarship.

"Vi . . ." The way her mom said it, her name sounded like a mistake.

"I'm sorry," Vi whispered. She wanted her mom to tell her it was okay. That she'd make it all go away.

But it was Nomi's mom who spoke. "We're going to figure this out," she promised. "Thank you for telling us."

ARTHUR

ARTHUR WAS LINGERING IN THE MUSEUM AFTER closing—sweeping the floors because he might as well be useful or something—when Lucas called.

"Don't tell." Lucas said, as soon as the video call started. He ran a hand over his head, his floppy hair temporarily blacking out Arthur's phone screen. "Obviously."

Arthur glanced back at the stairs, nerves racing as he imagined Danthony walking down. But no footsteps came.

He fumbled with his phone, turning the volume as low as he could before responding. "Tell what?" he asked, though he couldn't pretend, even to himself.

It was like the other guys on his team wanted to pretend everything was normal, but Arthur couldn't. Because here he was, *involved*, against all his best intentions.

Lucas rolled his eyes. "Vaughn called me into his office. I guess Vi made up some story about how I sent her picture to every guy at school."

"Oh man." The museum was too small. In the center of the room, those three blue-speckled vases stared at Arthur, waiting for his response. "Well I guess you . . . didn't, right? Send it to everyone? Like, showing people is different than sending it?"

"Obviously," Lucas repeated.

Obviously.

"Vaughn was freaked, though. You know he can't handle anything. He called my dad into the school. And Vi's and Nomi's moms, too. Over the top, really," Lucas continued. "But as long as we stick together, we'll all be fine. My dad won't let this ruin our lives."

"But didn't your dad say girls can ruin guys' lives?" The room went wobbly.

"Nah, he told Vaughn that Vi had a crush on me, and her ego's probably bruised because I didn't ask her to the dance. My dad's pretty sure she made stuff up because she's trying to get revenge."

"Okay . . ." Arthur couldn't tell if Lucas really believed that. The things Lucas's dad had said felt true before, but now—

"And the school can't do anything without proof," Lucas went on. "So keep quiet, stay out of it, and don't worry about a thing, Artsy."

But Arthur *was* worried about things, many of them, which was the whole problem.

Lucas hung up and Arthur's phone went dark, and he tried to breathe. The world really was hard for boys these days. Because if he said something, he could get in trouble, and his friends could get in trouble. And then would their lives be ruined?

But if he didn't say anything, what about the girls?

Did Nomi get expelled?

And what about Vi?

His friends had maybe kind of ruined *her* life, and then Nomi's by extension, and what was Arthur supposed to do about that?

He leaned against the vase stand—but he leaned with too much force, and the vases wobbled until one of them fell, almost in slow motion.

He watched it hit the floor and shatter, exploding in a thousand directions.

It was like the freaking *vase's* life flashed before his eyes. He pictured someone shaping it, painting it, leaving it on the museum stoop for his dad to find, imagining it would be loved and cared for, not destroyed by some careless kid—

And then he went back further, back to when the vase was still clay, still earth, pulled from the ground by human hands—

Whatever.

All of it, whatever.

He couldn't carry all of it, couldn't care about all his problems, and Nomi's problems, and Lucas's, and Vi's, and a forest full of smoke, and trees that felt pain, and also this *misshapen vase*.

It wasn't fair. It was too much.

The other two vases looked at him accusingly. Well.

He grabbed one of those vases and hurled it against the

wall, smashing it, destroying a painting of mushrooms in the process.

Good. Better. But not enough.

He took the final vase before it could protest and slammed it against the floor.

Who knew breaking could be so satisfying?

There were his dad's footsteps, finally, thundering into the museum. "Is everything"—Danthony stopped, staring at the shards and then at Arthur, who was panting like he'd just run a race in record time—"okay?"

Arthur stared at the mess he'd made. Only one way out of it, really. He opened his mouth to lie: *I don't know how this happened.*

But instead he broke, something crumbling inside him as tears fell, something built of clay and stone and earth.

A FEW YEARS AFTER A GIRL GAVE HIM TWO BOOKS, THE boy who calculated equations under our canopy walked by an art studio called From the Earth.

The studio was on Second and Madison, in a building that had been a hotel, once, and though humans don't always know the way earth holds memory, the way certain patches of soil welcome seeds over and over, sometimes they feel it.

As he walked by, the boy stopped.

He'd been frustrated. He'd just come from Pike Place Market and seen all the trinkets being passed off as Duwamish—handmade baskets and miniature "totem" poles, woven and carved by those without any ties to his culture, the legacy of his people repackaged and sold to the very people who had already stolen it.

To him, those poles felt like lies carved into our cedar bodies, and seeing them made him feel like he no longer belonged to himself. Like he needed to bend into a person others wanted him to be. And if he couldn't bend, he might as well break.

He was at a breaking point when he stopped on that corner of Second and Madison. Through the window, he saw speckled blue vases alongside large wooden carvings—and something inside him cracked. This was entirely different than Pike Place.

This feeling was new, blooming in that fractured part of his heart like a sprout rising through concrete. A need to make.

A seed.

A possibility.

VI

NOMI AND HER MOM CAME OVER TO VI'S HOUSE AFTER the meeting, to discuss their options, to debrief, to deconstruct every second of what just happened.

"This is outrageous," Nomi's mom kept saying, and Vi tried to gather some of that outrage, but she couldn't.

Everything was happening so fast, and she couldn't keep track of all the things she'd ruined.

It wasn't just that she couldn't trust Lucas anymore; it was that she couldn't trust herself.

Violet, what have you done?

Nomi had been standing, sitting, pacing, all in thirty-second intervals, like she couldn't figure out what to do with her body. "I'm so sorry, Mom," she said.

"Oh, Nomi," her mom whispered before taking her in her arms. She murmured into Nomi's ear, and though Vi couldn't hear, she imagined those scraps of comfort—that she was on Nomi's side, that she was proud, that Nomi had nothing to apologize for.

Vi looked at her own mom, who was wringing her hands, shaking her head like the world was crumbling.

Vi blurted, "I'm leaving Pineview too."

Her mom blinked. "Vi, honey. Why don't you take a breath—"

Vi took a breath. "I can't stay at that school. Not with Lucas there. Not without Nomi."

After Lucas and his dad had left that afternoon, Principal Vaughn brought Nomi, Vi, and the moms back into his office.

"We aren't expelling Nomi," he'd said, voice smooth and soothing in a grating kind of way. "We aren't expelling anyone."

Nomi's mom had placed a hand on his desk, leaning over. "If you take away her scholarship, you're effectively kicking her out. Which means my daughter gets punished more harshly because we don't have money. Whereas that boy gets to stay, scot-free, because he does."

In that stuffy office, Principal Vaughn had run a hand over his head. "We have no evidence—"

Nomi's mom jammed her finger at Vi. "*She* is your evidence."

Vi couldn't help but take that as an accusation.

Now, in Vi's living room, the moms fell silent, and Vi caught Nomi's eye. She expected Nomi to be happy that Vi was leaving too. Or at least a little less sad, but instead her friend went pale.

Vi's mom nodded slowly. "We can look into transferring you to another private school."

"Why can't I go to public school with Nomi?"

Her mom hesitated. "I . . ."

The air grew heavy with all the things they couldn't say. Nomi's mom flushed. Nomi looked down at her hands.

A ping cut through the silence, and Vi's mom grabbed her phone. "I'm so sorry." She turned to Nomi's mom. "I have to pick Blue up. Would you mind staying with the girls? I'll only be half an hour."

Nomi's mom gave one definitive nod, like she was shelving the awkwardness. "Of course."

"Thank you so much," her mom said before glancing back at her daughter. "Vi . . ."

Vi's heart beat. *Yes?*

But that was all her mom said before she left.

"I have to use the bathroom," Nomi said, standing abruptly and stumbling a little as she headed down the hall.

Nomi's mom looked down the hall, then back at Vi, like she was trying to decide if she could follow, if she could leave Vi alone.

"You should go to her," Vi said.

Nomi's mom started to leave, but hesitated. "What that boy did to you was wrong. I want you to know that."

"Yeah, but still . . . I know I shouldn't have sent it to him." Vi wondered if she'd be saying those words for the rest of her life. *I shouldn't have done it.* "I just . . . It was nice. He made me feel pretty. I thought he liked me, but now . . . I don't know."

She kept her eyes on the floor as her words rose into the air, impossible to take back. She wanted to turn to smoke and float up alongside them.

"Focus on what *you* feel, Vi," Nomi's mom said, softer. "Not *about* your body. *Inside* your body."

And then she went to follow her daughter, leaving Vi alone with her thoughts.

How did she feel inside her body? She turned the question over, searching for an answer. She'd been flipped inside out, for everyone's eyes except her own, and now what was left? What was there to see?

She found nothing, at first. But then—a spark.

Fire, she realized, smoldering and deep. There was something inside her that wanted to burn, glowing dimly now, but growing brighter, like a light in the distance, like the promise of warmth—and maybe she had to follow it.

NOMI

NOMI SHOVED HER WAY INTO THE DOWNSTAIRS BATHroom. It was too bright in there. Which made her headache worse.

She turned off every light except the glowing nightlight.

It was bad enough that Nomi couldn't go to Pineview anymore. But now Vi might not either! Because of Nomi! Everything had unraveled so quickly.

She leaned over the sink.

Then there was Vi's mom's response, like going to public school would be the worst thing in the world, which made Nomi feel entirely worthless! Her whole future was rushing down the drain and—

She turned on the water. Watched it gush from the faucet.

Her mom was keeping it together for Nomi. Vi was keeping it together for Nomi. So, in front of them, Nomi would keep it together, too.

But here? Alone? Panic swelled, threatening to drag her under. *Facts, facts, focus on what you know.*

Fact: Her scholarship was gone.

Fact: She couldn't attend Pineview without it.

She tried to wash her face, but her hands shook too much.

Fact: Shaking hands were a result of a triggered sympathetic nervous system—which, in fact, was entirely unhelpful information to know!

She rested her head on the marble countertop, polished to a gleam by the Kims' monthly housekeeper, who Vi never even saw because Vi's mom always made sure she and the kids were out of the house first.

The thought came up, as loud as it was unwelcome: *Vi is careless.* It skittered around her head like a roach, and she raced for it, trying to squash it.

It was an ugly thought, the kind of thing Principal Vaughn might think. Nomi shouldn't, couldn't, *wouldn't* think like that—especially not when Vi was willing to leave Pineview with her.

But still . . . as Nomi leaned her forehead against the cool marble counter, she couldn't help but think it was at least partially true.

Because Vi could *afford* to care less. She didn't have to worry, like Nomi did, constantly, about what came next. She didn't need to plan out the next ten years of scholarships, didn't need to worry about every single test, didn't even need to worry about smoke outside, because her parents bought expensive air filters that made their home safe.

Vi had all this protection, a canopy to shelter from storms, and Nomi didn't.

She didn't even have a *book*.

A knock at the door startled her, and she wasn't sure if she was ready to see Vi just yet, but it was her mom who said, "Nomi? You in there?"

For a second, Nomi was back in the bathroom at the dance, knocking on the door, asking about Vi—but now she was the one hiding.

Nomi felt ill. Her mom knocked again, and Nomi opened the door. "My head hurts," she said.

"Let me help." Nomi's mom slid inside, clicking the door shut before running a hand towel under warm water and pressing it to Nomi's brow. "Any better?"

"Marginally." Nomi sat on the lidded toilet, and her mom knelt beside her. "But my whole life plan is ruined, and a wet towel won't change that."

"Nomi . . . I know I've always preached the importance of a plan, but part of having a plan is knowing that things might not go exactly as you imagined." Her mom moved the towel down to Nomi's cheek. "I've been surprised many times in my life."

"Yeah," Nomi said, because she'd lived through the layoff and loss too. "And that's always been bad."

Her mom nodded slowly. "Sometimes the surprises have been challenging. But sometimes they're wonderful."

Nomi tried to believe that, but the evidence did not hold up. Her skepticism must have shown on her face, because her mom laughed. "I'm serious, Nomi. *You* have been the best surprise of my life."

"No," Nomi said, because she'd heard this story too, more than any other—about the doctors, and the tests, and the long years of wanting. "You planned for me. You worked so hard for me. And I tried to plan and work hard, too, but then I—"

"*Shh,* it's okay." Her mom lowered the towel. "I did plan for you, and I did work hard. I read every book. I talked to every doctor. I thought, after all those years, I was prepared. And you still surprised me—the day I found out you were in there, and every day after that. You surprise and delight me, always, with your humor and your passion and your *brain*. All of your Nomi-ness."

"Level Five Nomi," Nomi whispered.

Her mom pushed the hairs off her forehead, damp now from the towel. "And it's wonderful."

"Except when I'm tackling boys to the ground."

"Except for that."

"But he deserved it."

Her mom didn't agree—but she didn't *disagree* either.

Nomi sighed. "Maybe some surprises are okay," she conceded. "But not this one."

"You're right." Her mom took a very deep breath. "When we get home, we'll have a Nomi care day. We'll watch reality TV and eat cheesy pizza and fall down Wikipedia rabbit holes. And *then* we'll figure out what to do next. We'll make a plan for school."

Nomi nodded. There could be a plan. And it would still help. Even without the book.

She tried to make herself believe that.

"But right now," her mom continued, "Vi's going through a lot of bad too. Maybe you can lean on each other."

Nomi looked down at her palms. They were still shaking, which she hated. "I'm worried if I try to help, Vi will think I'm telling her how to be."

Her mom stood up. "Sometimes we don't need to tell people what to do," she said, as she offered Nomi a hand. "We don't need to have all the answers. We just need to be there."

VI

AS SOON AS NOMI STEPPED OUT OF THE BATHROOM, Vi dragged her upstairs. She wanted her best friend to herself.

"Are you okay?" Vi asked, clicking the bedroom door shut behind her.

Nomi flopped onto the bed. "Don't you think it's unfair, how some people have to care more than others?"

Vi joined Nomi, climbing on top of the blankets, that newfound fire still burning inside her. "Definitely. Like how girls have to care extra about what they look like." She nurtured the little flame. "Or how Blue has to care about the polar bears dying, even though she's only seven."

"Yeah," Nomi said, quieter, less Nomi than usual. "Or like my mom has to care about money."

And there it was—the thing unsaid. Vi was six the first time she went to Nomi's house, but even that young, even before Nomi's mom got laid off, Vi had recognized that Nomi had less money than she did. They'd never talked about it.

"I'm really sorry," Vi said. Apology, apology, apology. "I've ruined your scholarship, your life plan, and—"

"No," Nomi said. "It's Lucas's fault. And Vaughn's."

"I guess . . ." Vi looked up at that princess canopy, suddenly homesick for when she and Nomi were little. "Remember when we used to lie under the oak tree after school, and you'd make up stories about it?"

"Yeah," Nomi said softly. "I thought it was comforting to imagine secret messages carved in that tree. Like there were other people who had been there and knew how we felt and could look out for us. But that was silly."

"Not silly," Vi insisted. She understood the appeal: the idea that someone else had been in that very same spot and survived. "It's nice."

"Well, it's not based in reality. And speaking of things that aren't based in reality . . ." Nomi sat up, like she was discarding the conversation. "Come on."

Jumping off the bed, she pulled Vi's empty trash can out from under the desk and placed it on the comforter. "Let's put those awful drawings where they belong."

Vi sat up. Taking the drawings out meant having to see them again—but as soon as Nomi said it, Vi realized she didn't want to carry them anymore. She hadn't realized how heavy scraps of paper could be.

She grabbed her bag, dumped the contents, and watched the scraps flutter into the trash.

"There are more of them than I thought," Nomi murmured.

"Yeah," Vi said. They filled half the bin, those twisted versions of her, mocking her with their puffy lips and thick eyelashes.

"Do you feel any better?" Nomi asked.

Vi couldn't take her eyes off those stick figures. She was pretty sure they'd be burned into her brain forever. She was pretty sure she'd close her eyes at age ninety-three and still see them.

"No." That angry spark glowed. She was *not* going to carry this all the way to ninety-three. "I'll be right back."

She rushed from the room without waiting for Nomi's response. In the living room, Nomi's mom had her back turned, talking in hushed tones into her phone, about the law and privacy, and Vi slipped into the kitchen unseen.

She slid open a drawer, pocketed a tiny box, and returned to her bedroom, heart beating, skin hot.

She held the box out in her palm. "Matches."

"Oh," Nomi said, her face slowly splitting into a grin as she realized what Vi meant. "Awesome."

They rearranged themselves on the bed, hovering over the plastic trash can.

"I'm pretty sure witches do this," Nomi said. "Burn stuff."

Vi lifted a paper from the trash. She imagined the boys digging their pens across it, scrawling a spell of their own. *This is who we see. This is who you are.* "I thought witches got burned."

Nomi paused. "They weren't witches. Just women."

Vi inhaled as she pulled out a match. Exhaled as she struck it against the box.

The flame hissed to life, and Vi kissed it to the paper. Slowly, slowly, embers curled, devouring the stick-figure girl, and when the match burned low in her hand, flame creeping toward her fingerprints, she dropped it into the bin.

Fire spread, until each scrap was crumbling to ash.

Power. That was what she'd felt when she took the photo, and that was what she felt now, only now it was different. Then it had been fleeting, a grasp of a feeling before she sent it over to Lucas.

Now, it was hers.

"The fire should burn itself out," Nomi said.

The bin started melting. "Or maybe that only happens in metal cans," Nomi added.

Vi scrambled away from the fire, but the movement toppled the bin.

It tipped in slow motion, and then the flame ignited brighter, licking upward, tasting Vi's wooden bedpost, and then the canopy above it.

The girls leapt off the bed.

"Is that polyester?" Nomi asked.

The canopy began to burn.

Nomi screamed. Vi screamed. The fire roared.

"It's okay." Vi could hardly catch her breath. "The smoke alarm will automatically call the fire department."

"What smoke alarm?" Nomi cried.

And then Vi realized: The house was silent. The alarm had no batteries.

PART V

How do you turn a girl to flame?
When canopies burn, you'll never be the same.

FOR ALL THIS TALK OF FIRE, WE HAVEN'T TOLD YOU much about it.

Most fires die quickly, eating through our underbrush, warming our trunks without consuming. Some of those fires are welcome, lighting the forest to make it new again.

But others, the ones that burn to devour—those are the fires of nightmares. And when young seedlings ask the old growth for advice, we are at a loss.

We trees grow tall, the elders shielding the young from sun, so they spend years beneath our canopy, growing slow and strong.

But when that fails, when the young trees grow too fast, what can we say? We have nothing to give except for this:

Time is a ring. Listen. It might help you put the fire out.

NOMI

HOW DO YOU TURN A GIRL TO FLAME?

Some advice: Don't.

The hungry fire raced toward Vi's bedroom door. Did Nomi say hungry? She meant starving. Ravenous. Insatiable. *Et cetera.*

Nomi gulped for air. They were trapped in this room.

Fire ate oxygen. THEY WERE GOING TO RUN OUT OF OXYGEN.

THEY WERE GOING TO DIE.

Valiantly, Nomi rationed her final breaths, focusing so hard it took her a moment to realize Vi was shouting at her.

"Out the window. Down the trellis. Around the back to the living room window!" Vi said.

Calamity. Vi's brain must have already been losing oxygen. Poor Vi was losing her mind.

And then Nomi understood: a fire plan.

She hadn't realized how quickly she could move.

In less than a minute they were out the window, down

the trellis, and safely outside, and Nomi sprinted, slamming herself against the living room window.

Inside, her mom sat on the couch, totally unaware, holding her cooling mug in one hand and typing intently into her phone with the other.

"*Fire!*" Vi cried.

Nomi's mom looked up at them, startled.

"MOM!" Nomi screamed. Now, in fact, was exactly the time for Level 5 Nomi. "GET OUT OF THE HOUSE RIGHT NOW!"

Her mom dropped the mug.

VI

VI'S MOM ARRIVED WITH BLUE AFTER THE FIRE TRUCKS.

So at least there was that. At least Blue didn't have to see the flames she'd been fearing for months. Vi's room was charred, but the rest of the house was okay, aside from the water damage and the intense smell of smoke clinging to the air.

Seeing the drenched house, her mom burst from the car without closing the door and raced toward Vi, grabbing her. "Thank god," she murmured. "Thank god."

Vi let herself be held, sinking into the moment and letting it stretch. She felt like a little kid, but maybe that was okay.

Eventually, her mom left to talk to the firefighters, and while Nomi huddled with her own mom, Vi climbed into the back seat of her car. Her little sister sat paralyzed, skin glowing red in the flashing emergency lights.

"It happened," Blue whispered.

She hadn't even taken off her seat belt, so Vi unclipped it and scooted closer until their arms touched.

"It was my fault," Vi said.

Blue looked at her, eyes wide, and Vi nearly doubled over with big-sister guilt.

"But everything's okay." Vi said. "I'm okay. We're okay. And you know what? Your fire plan saved us. *You* saved us."

Blue's words were barely audible. "I did?"

Well, the plan had certainly helped, and Vi didn't need to tell Blue about the whole fire-alarm-batteries thing. "You did."

"And you're okay," Blue repeated, like that was a marvel. She pushed her little body closer, and then she threw her arms around Vi, squeezing tight.

Vi could barely breathe. Who knew her little sister had so much strength? "I'm here," Vi promised.

"I know," Blue said. "I'm just making sure."

Vi felt that amber feeling again, like she wanted to shield Blue from everything.

But then Blue started to laugh. "You set the house on fire!" she cried, almost hysterical.

And then Vi started to laugh too. Maybe she was also a little hysterical. "Not on purpose!"

"Don't do that again."

"Never."

Blue loosened her grip. "It's kinda hard to hold on that tight."

"Yeah," Vi said, something in her heart hurting.

Blue pulled back and looked up at her sister, and here

was Blue: still breathing, still bright, eyes shining like she'd just discovered something.

Because what do you do when your biggest fear comes true?

What do you do when it comes true—and the world still turns?

ARTHUR

THE LOCKER ROOM AFTER A WIN ALWAYS MADE Arthur's head spin. It was like nowhere else. His team was jumping, slamming lockers, knocking into one another because there was no other way to express this level of joy. It had been a small weekday meet hosted by Pineview, pared down thanks to air quality, but that didn't matter to anyone because they'd run so well. Their legs were on fire and nobody could touch them and the world belonged to them and whatever—Arthur didn't want it.

Lucas slapped him on the back. "Artsy! You ran almost as good as me!"

Yes, he had, around and around the indoor track because *still* with the freaking smoke, and it had done nothing to smother the burn inside him.

The other guys were talking, shouting, whooping like they'd just conquered a city.

"Hey," Lucas pulled Arthur aside. "You push yourself too hard again?"

"No," Arthur said. Would this feeling ever go away?

This crushing feeling like he'd done something wrong and was destined to *always* do it wrong, again and again?

He couldn't live like this. There had to be a way out, a way to breathe.

"Sorry, my dad's here," he said as he pulled his phone out of his cross-country bag. Danthony didn't mind waiting; he was used to it, since Arthur never skipped out on the post-running high. But now Arthur needed that time for something else.

Nomi was still suspended. She hadn't been in school today, or yesterday. Neither had Vi.

He texted his dad: **Be there in fifteen.**

Lucas gripped his shoulder, a little too hard. "Okay. Take care, man."

And maybe he was just being supportive, but the statement felt loaded. *Take care of yourself. Take care of us. Don't do anything we'll all regret.*

Arthur forced a grin. "Will do."

He jogged across campus, toward the admin building, trying not to choke on smoke. It was already four-thirty, and part of him was hoping Vaughn was gone—

But when he stepped into the building, he found the principal sitting in his office with his door wide open.

Arthur didn't get involved, as a general rule. He'd always believed that made things worse.

Except he *was* involved—with Vi's picture, with the book of prophecies, and even, in his small way, with the stolen land and the burning forest and the whole freaking planet.

He hadn't asked for it, but here he was, in this place, in this life, so, sure. If he was already involved, he'd do it his way.

He walked into Vaughn's office without letting himself doubt and blurted the words.

"Lucas showed me Vi's picture," he said. "He showed all of us."

IF FIRE IS HEAT BUILDING, MOUNTING TO UNDENIABLE, how do you put the fire out?

If fire is a ring, a cycle of bigger and hotter, the past racing toward the future, how do you put the fire out?

If fire is a story, roaring loud, begging you to listen, listen.

There's a story humans tell, in circles and circles, about a tree that gives and a human who takes.

It's a true story. It happens all the time.

But it's not the only story.

ARTHUR

AS ARTHUR CLIMBED INTO HIS DAD'S CAR AFTER TALKing to Vaughn, he felt sick. His head pounded.

"Your principal just called me," Danthony said. He sat with his hands in his lap, not even bothering to start the engine.

"I know," Arthur responded. His own voice felt very far away. He could barely hear it over the pounding. "He said he would."

Silence, except for the *bumbumbum* behind his brows.

"I had no idea any of this was happening," Danthony said.

When Danthony had asked about the broken vases, Arthur said the smoke was getting to him. That he missed running outside. That he was so tired of living in the haze.

It hadn't been a total lie, but it was only a tiny shard of truth.

Now, Arthur waited for a lecture. He was too tired to feel defensive. But instead Danthony said, "I'm really proud of you."

Maybe Arthur should have felt proud too, but he felt empty. The burn had faded, and now he was burned out.

When would Lucas find out what Arthur did? What about the rest of his team?

Running was the only thing that kept Arthur sane, and now he could never go back. He buried his face in his arms. Into his elbows, he confessed: "Sometimes it's like I don't know where to step."

A pause, and then Arthur felt his dad's warm hand on his back.

"The big secret is, we all kind of feel that way. So much of life is figuring out each step as it comes: What's happening in our world, and how do we best respond to it?" Danthony said. "But it's okay to ask for help, too. You can always, always ask Abba and me."

"I know." Arthur kept his head down. "But I just feel like everything I say and do is wrong. Maybe boys *are* bad. Maybe guys just break things."

"Oh, Arthur. I never want you to feel like that. It's not true." Danthony took a deep breath. "Some men in power *have* broken things, big things. And people are frustrated about that. *I'm* frustrated about that. But none of that frustration should be directed at *you*. Some people do make generalizations. But that's not right, either. You're your own person. You get to make your own decisions and pick your own path, and so far you've navigated it admirably."

Arthur lifted his head. Part of him wanted to push his

dad's words away, because that answer felt too hard and too easy at the same time. But it also made him feel a little better, and Arthur let himself believe it might be true.

Danthony started the car. "How about you shower and eat a quick dinner at home?" he said. "Then there's somewhere I want to take you. It's called From the Earth."

BY 1995, FROM THE EARTH HAD BECOME AN ART STUDIO. It was a safe place where young people could learn to make art, started by a husband and wife, a Duwamish carver and a Swedish potter.

The boy with a seed in his heart, the boy who once did his homework under our canopy, went there almost every day.

He learned to carve from the man with skin as weathered and brown as oak, and as he did, he discovered his roots, learned with a block of wood and a knife to face the rings of the past, to speak back to them and find his place inside them.

This, he thought. *This is what learning can be.*

And then, as the old carver showed him how to tell his own story, as the boy reclaimed himself in the process, the boy thought, *That is what teaching can be.*

The old carver was dreaming up a project for the future, a citywide art installation. Before settlers burned Duwamish villages, all those years before, a hundred longhouses had decorated the land, many of them structurally supported by story poles—homes held up by cedar-carved history.

In this dream of a project: What if they never burned? What if those story poles were still there? Maybe not a hundred—he couldn't carve that many—but enough to be a reminder, a resurrection, a refusal to be erased or forgotten.

The boy visited the studio once a week, watching the project develop.

Decades passed. The boy became a man, graduated from high school, then college, then found a job that filled him with joy—and through all that, he continued to carve.

One day, as he cleaned out his house to make room for a new project, he unboxed a pair of journals. He'd forgotten he had them, given to him by an old friend, a girl who'd become a professor.

He'd never really understood those books. They'd always felt, to him, like *part* of a story. Never the whole. But looking at them now, a feeling churned inside him—a forest, a chorus, asking to be born anew. Perhaps he could add to the story.

Back in the studio, his teacher's project was coming to an end, and when his teacher asked for help on the final pole, the man flipped through the second book for inspiration.

Time is a circle, it read. *Seeing is a flower. Breathe.*

VI

"THANKS FOR SPENDING THE DAY WITH ME," HER MOM said.

"Sure," Vi responded. Her mom had let her skip school again, and they'd planned a "bonding day," because that was what it seemed like they should do, but it had been awkward.

They'd spent a few hours shopping (unsuccessfully), seen a movie (Vi hadn't paid much attention), eaten diner-food dinner (grilled cheese), and were now sipping the dregs of their milkshakes as they milked time before going home.

Or, rather, going to their hotel. Their home was fine, or at least it would be, but they had to be out of the house while they waited for the smell of smoke to dissipate and a construction crew to rebuild Vi's room.

Vi's dad had been upset about the fire, but that paled in comparison to his reaction to the photo. There'd been a very tense, hushed conversation between her parents, just outside the hotel-room door, and Vi had sat on the pull-out couch with Blue, her dread mounting.

When her dad came back in, he sat Vi down.

I should be more present for you, he'd said, and she hadn't known how to respond. She'd believe it when it happened, but if it was true, that might be nice.

Now, in the diner, her mom looked up and said, "I messed up."

Vi almost choked on her milkshake. "What?"

"With the Instagram account. You'll . . ." She shook her head. "I want to say you'll understand when you're older, but maybe you already do."

Vi wasn't sure she wanted to understand. She focused on her straw, swirling rings into her drink, around and around.

"When people see you the way you want to be seen—when you feel like you can *control* how you're seen—it's hard to resist. And with *Raising Wildflowers*, people see me as a good mom. As a mom who makes some mistakes, sure, but overall: *good*. But I . . ." She ran a hand through her hair, which she hadn't blow-dried like usual. "I'm not certain that's true."

After Lucas screenshotted the photo, Vi thought she'd have to apologize to everyone. But instead, everyone was apologizing to *her*—Arthur, her mom, her dad, Nomi. "It's fine, Mom."

"No." Her mom took a determined breath, like she was about to say something she'd practiced. "In trying to control how people saw *me*, I took away your agency over how people saw you."

Emotion rose in Vi's throat. She swirled her straw faster, rings becoming a whirlpool.

"So I deleted all the photos of you and Blue from the account," her mom continued. "I won't post about you anymore. I hope you'll forgive me."

Vi stopped swirling. Her eyes snapped to her mom's. She'd never had the power to forgive an adult before, let alone one of her parents.

"And I'm going to therapy," her mom added. "In fact, we're both gonna go to therapy."

"Seriously?" Vi asked, but it was more of a reflex than anything else. In truth, it didn't seem so bad.

"We'll find you someone you trust," her mom promised.

Vi hesitated before nodding. "Fine. But you should find someone for Blue, too. She falls asleep by making disaster plans."

"She makes disaster plans? I thought it was just the alarms. And the polar bears. And the wildfires." Her mom sighed. "Therapy will be good."

Her mom's phone rang, and her brows rose when she glanced at the screen. "It's your principal."

"Oh." Vi's chest went cold as her mom slid out of the booth and walked to a quiet side of the diner.

From the distance, Vi could only make out murmurs of the call, and she tried not to strain. It was going to be okay. Or, if not *okay*, then it couldn't possibly get worse. Maybe Vaughn had decided to believe her, or maybe he was calling to say he did not. Vi didn't care about anything he said unless he decided to give Nomi back her scholarship.

She turned toward the window to distract herself, and

through the smoke-gray world, her gaze landed on a carved wooden pole outside. One of those story poles. She'd seen a couple of them before, so she knew about the art installation, poles bursting up from the pavement like trees with something to say.

This one had rings, faces carved into circles, and animals reaching toward the sky, and there was something about it that knocked into Vi. It demanded to be seen. It demanded to exist in this space without apology.

As she stared, a feeling unfurled inside her. It tasted like . . . it tasted like . . . she wasn't sure, exactly.

"He told you?" Her mom's voice rose, cutting through the diner, and Vi leaned forward. Lucas? Had Lucas said something?

Her mom hung up and slid back into the booth, slightly out of breath, cheeks flushed, like she'd been running.

"What happened?" Vi asked. Maybe she did care what Vaughn had to say.

"Arthur spoke to him," her mom said as she set her phone on the table, "which means the school finally has evidence. And Lucas won't be at Pineview anymore."

NOMI

NOMI HAD STAYED HOME FROM SCHOOL FOR TWO days, on account of the suspension, and on account of she couldn't bear being there anyway.

But come Friday, she donned her backpack and pushed her way through the heavy doors of Pineview. She'd only be here until winter break. Arthur had confessed, and Lucas's dad was arranging for Lucas to be transferred to a different private school. But despite all that, Vaughn hadn't changed his mind about the scholarship. Nomi's violence was an *unrelated issue*, and even though it made Nomi want to scream and cry at the same time, apparently she couldn't do anything about it.

School itself was not as bad as Nomi had anticipated. Thanks to the bizarre rumor that Vi and Nomi had actually burned *Lucas's* house down, her classmates gave them space, shooting them wary and fascinated glances.

Nomi didn't care. Or at least she cared *less*. And she might have been imagining it, but she could've sworn a few of her classmates' looks were approving. Alice Thorton, the girl with the not-see-through skirt, passed them in the hallway, and when Nomi waved, she waved back.

Nomi could bear this, she decided.

The worst class of the day was math, where she sat with her head buried in her textbook, avoiding her classmates' whispers and Mr. Romero's eyes. Lucas was still there, because he wasn't transferring until next week, but thankfully he kept his head down too. Somehow, she managed to survive the hour, but as she was getting ready to bolt after class, Mr. Romero asked her to stay behind.

Some other students slowed their pace, attempting to eavesdrop, but he waited for them to leave before speaking. "Principal Vaughn filled me in on what happened," he said. "It would be unprofessional of me to speak poorly of another student, and it would be even worse of me to condone violence. To be very clear, I do not."

"Of course not." Nomi tried to push the rising lump back down her throat. On top of everything else, losing her favorite teacher was too much.

"But your reason for doing it is not lost on me. Your frustration, your anger, your loyalty to your friend—none of those are misplaced."

She was startled by the softness in his voice. "Thanks," she managed.

In response, he pulled a pamphlet from his desk drawer and held it out. "There are a lot of great teachers in Seattle's public schools. Good programs, too."

Nomi took the pamphlet, running her fingers along

the title. *University of Washington Outreach: Young Seedlings, Blooming Botanists.*

And then, beneath it: *"The Things We Don't Yet Know"— A program for promising young scientists to engage with nature's beautiful mysteries. Led by Professor Newman.*

Professor Newman.

Nomi's heart caught as she read the name again and again.

"An old friend of mine started the program," Mr. Romero said. "She's brilliant."

Nomi nearly dropped the pamphlet. "You know her?"

Her teacher pointed toward the front of the school. "We used to sit under that Garry oak together, the one by the pickup. Back when I was a scholarship student here."

Nomi's fingertips spindly-tingled. The hair on the back of her neck stood up. Her future was unknowable, but this was *something*. Maybe it was fate, written in the stars, or the trees.

Or maybe it was just a coincidence.

"I've talked with Principal Vaughn," Mr. Romero continued. "You're a bright student. You're a good friend. You deserve opportunities, even when you make a mistake. So rest assured that the altercation with Lucas won't go on your permanent record. And if you need any help when it comes to high school applications, I'll be here."

Nomi stared at the pamphlet, then looked back up at him and felt something rising inside her.

Maybe she had a canopy after all.

IN 2021, A YOUNG WOMAN HAD STARTED TAKING pottery classes at From the Earth, and she was enchanted by the way a flaming kiln could turn earth into art.

She was just a few months into her first job out of college, an assistant at Amazon, and her boss had given her control over one of the digital billboards. *This is a big marketing opportunity,* he'd said. *Write nice messages.* He'd meant nice messages about the company, but she'd taken it to mean poetry. It felt like a rebellion of sorts, to write something beautiful on a sign meant for advertising.

She lifted her first set of bowls from the kiln. Fire had hardened her clay and given it shine, and she admired her work. The bowls were mishappen. She'd only be able to eat out of one of them. But the others were deserving, still, of being seen.

Luckily, there was a museum for art lost and found, and as she tucked her lopsided bowls into a box, as she turned to leave the studio, she saw two books abandoned by a beautifully carved pole.

One of the books was still in good condition, the other crumbling with age, but as she flipped through their pages, poetry stirred inside her. *These deserve to be seen too,* she thought. So she tucked some of the phrases into her heart, saving them for her billboard. Then she tucked the books into the box.

It was a short walk to the museum, only a block away, and she left the bowls and the books on its doorstep, like seeds scattered to the wind, ready to be found.

VI

VI HAD HATED PLAYING PIANO, BUT DISCOVERY OF ALL discoveries, she actually liked listening to it. Her earbuds pumped climactic chords straight into her veins, and as she walked toward their tree by the pickup, at the end of her first day back at school, she felt like she could breathe again, despite the smoke.

And then she saw Lucas.

He was standing alone by the curb, just out of reach of the oak's shadow, and her heart gave that same kick-drop of a crush, because even though her brain knew for certain that she hated him forever, her body hadn't yet gotten the memo.

She pulled her hoodie up over her hair, ready to flee—but she stopped.

She wasn't the one who should hide. He didn't get to decide not to care.

She pocketed her earbuds and pulled her hood back down before walking up to him. If he and his friends were going to burn her, then fine, she'd become fireproof.

He looked up, a flash of fear in his eyes. *Good.*

"Hi," she said, which was not really the intimidating opening she'd hoped for.

"Hey," he responded.

Despite the hundreds of texts they'd exchanged, this was their first time talking in person. Vi didn't have a plan for this conversation, but as soon as she started, she knew she had to ask. It was the embarrassing question she'd had since it happened.

"Was any of it real?" she asked.

He stepped back, almost imperceptibly. "I don't know what you mean."

Vi swallowed hard. She would not let him hurt her anymore. *Fireproof.* "Why'd you show them?"

He didn't say anything, but Vi could see the emotions fighting beneath his expression. Somehow, despite herself, she still wanted access to them. But he shrugged. "Same reason you showed me."

Clearly he had no idea why she'd shown him, and she'd never tell him because it was so embarrassing. Even more embarrassing than the picture itself.

She'd wanted to be someone *special*. She'd wanted to be worthy.

And then he'd responded with the biggest *you're not*, and he hadn't cared if that broke her.

"Say sorry," she said, voice cracking, nearly begging.

Of all the people apologizing to her, *he* was the one who

should. She deserved that. At the very, very least, he could give her that.

He opened his mouth, and Vi's whole body tensed, waiting-dreading-hoping all at once.

"Say it," she whispered.

For a moment, she thought he would. For a moment, it was just them and their secrets, and the taste of honey had soured and would never be sweet again, but maybe, maybe his apology would ease some of the swirling horror.

Then his dad's BMW pulled up, shiny windows tinted black so nobody could see inside. Lucas looked at the car, then back at her for one lingering second.

Say it, she thought.

But instead, he left, escaping into another world, where he didn't have to say a thing.

Vi stood there on the sidewalk, watching the car peel away, and she felt ridiculous. Even after all he'd done she'd still expected something from him, still thought he could give her something.

Shaking, halfway to crying, she shoved her earbuds back in, turning the volume up until it hurt. An entire orchestra swelled around her, and she looked up to see the branches of the tree.

Years ago, so far into the past it seemed like a different lifetime, that tree had felt like a whole hidden world, a sanctuary that saw everything and everyone.

Without questioning, without telling herself no, she

ripped off the too-hot hoodie. It didn't suit her, really, and neither did the ruffled top she wore underneath, but that didn't matter much.

She jumped, throwing herself onto the lowest branch, and her arms scraped as the bark caught her. She pushed herself up, and she couldn't remember the last time she'd climbed a tree, but now that she'd started, she didn't want to stop.

Briefly, she remembered the prophecy: *When leaves flutter, too high to climb, too far to fall.* But that future was past now. She was making her own way. Blood pumped through her limbs, and she felt her soul settle back into her body as she reached up, and then up again, like she was reaching toward the person she might become.

She climbed past knots and branches, higher and higher, until she found sharp letters, carved into the bark.

The words: *I was here.*

She ran her fingers over them. She, Nomi, and Arthur had imagined a message like this when they were younger, and now here it was, here it had been, hovering over them the whole time.

Her senses flooded. She was here.

She tasted that unexpected flavor again, the one she'd tasted when she looked at the story pole—and now it tasted like a revelation. Like something new. Like cedar, like spice, like a chill in the air, the temperature dropping on the first cold day in fall.

And it didn't taste like a secret.

Finally, she let herself look down at the school, and dizziness rocked her, but she wrapped her arms tighter around the tree.

She'd spent so much time worrying about how people might see her, but this was Vi, seeing. Seeing was a flower, seeing was Vi, Violet, whatever name she chose for herself, seeing was hers.

The school looked smaller from that height. And she felt bigger, with her hands rubbed bark-raw and her ears swelling with piano chords.

Lucas was leaving, and so was Nomi, and eventually, Vi would too. Maybe part of her would stay rooted there, long after, in that moment. But like her tree, she'd grow. Like her tree, she'd survive.

WE TREES KNOW OF FIRE—BUT WHAT COMES AFTER?

Some of us are built to resist, with bark so thick only the hottest flames can test us.

But thick skin only gets you so far, and when the hottest fires burn, reducing a forest to smoke, the only thing left to do is regrow.

Aboveground, there's only ash. But don't forget our roots, nutrients saved, memories stored, ready to press up again and taste the future.

There are seeds waiting too, scattered in a fiery wind, survivors ready to start anew. Some of us still—ask the lodgepole pine—are made for fire, with pine cones that only flames can open.

It is possible to grow after a burn. It is even possible to grow back stronger.

ARTHUR

A POTTERY CLASS.

That was what had been so urgent to Danthony, the place he believed Arthur needed to go. From The Earth—FTE—the name of an art studio. Danthony suspected the vases had come from there and, as he told Arthur, it's okay to break sometimes. But it might feel even better to build.

At first, when Arthur walked into the studio that smelled like purified mud, he'd turned to walk right out.

But Danthony stopped him. "Their pottery class is every Tuesday night for six weeks," he'd said. "Try it tonight, and then you can choose if you want to continue."

So Arthur sat on one of the low stools, felt the earth against his palms, watched it spin in circles and circles, around and around—and unlike the racing rings of the track, there was something about this that slowed his mind. It was grounding.

To Arthur's surprise, he did want to continue.

He was two weeks in, and he kept finding dried clay on

his elbows, like the earth was clinging to him, unwilling to let go.

One evening, as he was displaying his first clay creation in his dad's museum—a tiny cup that looked a little like a melted pine cone—he heard the door chime and looked up to see Nomi.

The breath went out of him. He was so surprised he nearly knocked his art right over.

She cleared her throat. He cleared his.

"I like that," she said, nodding toward the cup.

He frowned, studying her face for signs of sarcasm, but Nomi had never been the type for mockery. "It's a cup," he explained. "But it doesn't look great. It's . . . lumpy."

She shrugged. "I like it."

"You *do*?" He flushed hot, which was ridiculous. It wasn't like she was talking about *him*. She had no idea he'd made it.

"What?" Nomi asked. "You hate it?"

"No. I mean. No."

She was looking at the thing he'd made like it was something worth seeing.

Maybe it wasn't *so* silly that people left their art here.

"Um, how's your fall break been?" he asked, because he could not ask, *What are you doing here?* And he could not say, *I'm sorry you have to leave Pineview.*

She shrugged, which was fine, because it was a useless question anyway.

"I'm sorry you have to leave Pineview," he said, because,

whatever, he was tired of not saying things, and he really did feel that way.

"Yeah." She broke his gaze, twisting her hands together. "Sorry you couldn't finish the cross-country season. I heard you quit."

"Yeah." He wanted to tell her he'd be okay, because he would. He'd run again on his own, and he might join the team in high school. Who knew, he might even join again next year—maybe being with the team would be easier without Lucas. But telling her that felt like rubbing his okayness in.

"Thanks for telling Vaughn," she said. "For Vi's sake."

"I wish . . ." He could have helped Nomi, too. "You know, your scholarship."

"Yeah."

"Yeah."

So awkward. And yet talking to her was kinda nice, too. She'd barely looked at him since the dance.

He smiled at her. She smiled back. And something happened in his chest. It was different from the addictive, awful swooping feeling, halfway between fascination and fear.

This feeling was almost warm.

She unzipped her backpack and pulled out the old book, holding up the weathered pages that had meant so much to her. "I wanted to bring this back. Vi and I were gonna talk about it for our social studies project, but that felt wrong. So we're talking about the story poles instead."

"Right." The social studies project, the whole lie they'd

concocted to work together. He hadn't even considered what he'd actually do for that, but he'd figure it out later. Maybe he'd talk about the museum.

He walked over until he was standing right in front of her, then decided he'd gotten too close, then took a big step back, then decided he'd made it weird. "Right," he repeated.

Nomi cleared her throat. "It feels like, I don't know, like we're not supposed to have it anymore."

He stared at the book that had brought them together once, and then twice, and wanted to protest. But Nomi was right, as usual. The prophecies had already come and passed. For whatever came next, they were on their own.

But, still. It didn't feel right to just stop caring. "We should do something with it, though."

She ran her fingers over the cover before looking back up at him. "Like what?"

The past month, even as she'd softened to him, she'd rarely asked him a question. If she did, she asked it like a challenge, daring him to know the answer. Even before their friendship ended, her questions had often felt rhetorical, like she was only half listening to the response. The rest of her was busy chasing the answer in her own head.

But this time, she asked him simply. Like she really cared what he thought. It wasn't a dare, and it didn't feel like a burden. It felt like an invitation. He was part of this too.

He accepted the invitation.

"I have an idea," he said, growing excited as it formed. "But we need Vi."

Nomi hesitated.

"Trust me," he said.

She chewed her lip, deciding. Then nodded. "I'll ask her," she said, turning to go, but he couldn't just let her leave, not without saying something.

"Nomi, wait." He had to make some big, grand confession of, well, whatever. Like in the movies. "This is for you."

He handed her his melted, lumpy, clay cup, and then instantly regretted it. He wasn't sure what propelled him to offer it up, except that her question had almost felt like a gift, and he wanted to give her one in return. Level the playing field. Or something.

"What?" she asked. "You want me to take that?"

"Um . . . please? If you want?" He winced, trying to think of a way to undo the last five seconds, but she took it from him and nestled it into her jacket pocket.

"Thanks," she said. "If you're sure that's okay."

Say something good, he thought. *Make it less awkward.*

He churned through about a million phrases in his head, none of them quite right, but then the window behind him caught his attention, and he felt a shift inside him, like an exhale.

"Nomi," he said. "It's raining."

PART VI

WHAT DO TREES KNOW OF RAIN?

We wait and we wait, and eventually, it comes.

It always comes.

Time is not a circle, but a ring, and we trees build rings year by year, layer by layer. The new bark doesn't know every scar buried in its core. But each past ring is a promise to the future, centering the new growth, supporting it, singing as rain races down its grooves. The past whispers to the present, if it's willing to listen:

Soak it in.

Now, on the corner of First and Madison, a girl steps out of a museum with a tree clutched to her chest and the earth tucked in her pocket. She stops, enjoying the long-awaited rain as it soaks her clothes, but she holds the book close, shielding it.

She's not the kind of kid who believes in magic, but on days like these, a part of her wonders.

On days like these, it's as if the world has something to

say, as if words rise from the soil, the flowers, the leaves—like the trees themselves want to be poets.

If she could hear us—which someday she might—we'd tell her it's not magic. The book in her arms, the advice and thoughts and poetry collected from so many, that's just words.

Except, of course, when somebody needs to hear them.

NOMI

IT RAINED ALL DAY AND ALL NIGHT, AND NOMI COULDN'T get enough. As it turned out, rain had a *smell*—fresh and clear and cold, like ice in her lungs. And her *lungs*—it was like she'd been filling them halfway, and she'd forgotten how much deeper she could breathe.

The next morning, she called Vi.

"It smells like *trees*," Nomi said, forgetting the whole point of the call. "Did you know trees had a smell?"

Vi just laughed. "Of course trees have a smell."

But Nomi hadn't known! Or she hadn't noticed. Maybe those were the same thing.

Vi came over, and they stood outside until their hair dripped into their eyes. If their lives were a movie, music might have swelled: a song, "Dancing Queen," maybe. But there, in that moment, the only noise was the rain and the rush of cars and the sound of Vi laughing.

Nomi wanted to stay in that moment forever. She wanted to drink the air. But time kept turning, and she remembered what she was supposed to say. "Arthur wants us to meet. About the book."

Vi closed her eyes and tipped her face to the sky.

"But you don't have to," Nomi went on, "if you don't want to. I know the book—I know you don't care as much as me—I'm not saying you should—and I know you might not want to see Arthur—I'm not saying you should—"

"I care." Vi opened her eyes to look at Nomi. "I'll be there."

The rain continued for another week, and the kids met the evening it finally stopped.

Outside, a pink wash of sunset broke through the overcast gray sky.

Inside, Nomi, Arthur, and Vi huddled in Arthur's living room around an old book of prophecies. Or poems. Or scraps of ideas. Who was to say?

"I just," Arthur started, flushing again, "I thought we should say goodbye to the book or whatever. I don't know, it seemed like the book was helping us. And I thought, if some kids find it after us, we could . . ." He nudged the book toward Nomi and handed her a pen.

"We could add something for them, too," Nomi finished, understanding dawning—quicky followed by concern. "But how do we know what to write? We don't know the future."

"No, but we can still be helpful." Vi cleared her throat. "Here's something: Don't send pictures in your bra."

Arthur and Nomi froze, but then Vi laughed. "What? It's good advice."

Nomi had not realized Arthur could go quite so red. She wrote: *Careful with pictures.*

As she scratched the pen against a blank spot of paper, she expected to feel like she was doing something wrong. But she didn't.

"What else?" she asked.

Arthur offered, "Running in smoke hurts your lungs. The indoor track is better sometimes, even if it's not as fun."

Nomi nodded. *Take the indoor track when you need to.*

Vi added, "Pay attention to story poles."

"Say yes to the group project," Arthur said.

"Classical music isn't bad," Vi suggested.

Arthur frowned. "Is this advice any good?"

Nomi wrote *Pay attention to stories* and *Say yes* and *Hear the music.*

"What about you, Nomi?" Vi asked.

Nomi set the pen down. It was an impossible amount of pressure, that was the problem. The book felt like—well, *fine*, she'd just say it—it felt like magic.

And they were just them.

But that was the thing. The book wasn't just about them, at least not entirely. *Rings of memory,* the professor had said.

The book had included them, for a moment, but it was bigger than them, in that spindly-tingling way. It was like there was a connectedness, a canopy, a *feeling* that extended beyond what she could know or see.

Now was their turn to pass that feeling on. They didn't have to be magic themselves. They just had to let themselves be part of magic.

So Nomi pictured herself standing on the edge of the future.

She could tell future kids that the world was burning, but there were ways to put the fire out. She could tell them that everything would be okay.

But that didn't seem quite right. She was still figuring the future out for herself. She didn't know what came next, so she didn't have much to give the future except, maybe, one thing.

She picked the pen back up, brought it to paper, and wrote, like words carved into a tree:

> We were here.
> And we'll be here.

A fact. And even a promise.

AUTHOR'S NOTE

Here's a promise, dear reader: For every copy of this book sold, I will donate a portion of my net proceeds to Earthjustice, an organization that protects and defends the environment. Another promise: Random House, the publisher, has made a donation to One Tree Planted, so that new trees will be planted in honor of this book.

It feels urgent to do this, because we live in urgent times.

As I write this, on the morning of September 17, 2025, I'm sitting in my home in Seattle, watching the haze roll in. A hundred miles from here, the North Cascades National Park is on fire, lit up by ever-increasing global heat, and smoke blankets the city.

The world is on fire. Some of those fires are literal. Others are metaphorical—they can't be doused with water alone. And watching them all rage, it's hard not to feel worried or angry or scared. It's hard to breathe.

I don't know when or where you're reading this book. Maybe you're curled up in bed, decades into the future. Maybe in that future these worries are a distant past. I hope so. But maybe this book has found you at a time when you, too, are looking out at a world on fire and asking, *How do we live in it?*

When I was a kid asking that question, adults either told me there was nothing to be done, or that my generation would fix the world. Both of those answers felt impossible to carry. And neither of them turned out to be true.

I want you to know: There are things we can do.

And, more importantly: It's not all on you to do it. It's not all on you to save the world.

Because what I found as I got older was that change is a work in progress. So many people, across so many generations, have been doing that work. And I could be a part of it.

I dedicated this book to my community because I know and love so many people who show up, every day, to make the world a better place. Whether it's advocating for clean energy, protecting communities from climate disaster, giving kids a safe place to play after school, planting gardens for pollinators, feeding the hungry, building homes for the poor, protesting for peace, or standing up for kids' freedom to read—I have met a whole forest's worth of people who are trying to help. I'm sure you have as well, maybe without even realizing it.

The truth is, there's no easy answer to how we live in a world on fire. But if I had to give one, I would say: *together.* So many of us are working hard, together. And one day, when you're ready, we will need your help, too. But you won't be alone.

It's the forest, not the trees. We are here, and we'll be here.

That's my promise.

With care,

ACKNOWLEDGMENTS

Though I can't give readers easy answers, I hope this book offers a resting place for big feelings and big questions. I hope this book shelters readers while they need it, and then, when they're ready, invites them into the canopy.

To teachers, librarians, and educators—thank you for being such an important part of kids' communities. Thank you for shepherding them through the pain, and for guiding them into their power.

I could fill a whole forest with thank-yous, but I'll try to keep them to a few pages.

To Caroline Abbey, the perfect editor for this book, thank you for trusting me to write about a Greek chorus forest, climate anxiety, prophecies, and a certain kind of photo without ever asking *Are you sure that's a good idea?* Thank you for helping me find my way to The End.

Thank you to Tiff Liao for supporting this story as it

became a real book; to Katrina Damkoehler, for refusing to give up on the cover quest; and to the rest of the team at Random House Children's Books—Barbara Marcus, Mallory Loehr, Jasmine Hodge, Megan Shortt, Havilah Sciabbarrasi, Kelly McGauley, Adrienne Waintraub, Katie Halata, Katie Dutton, Erica Trotta, Kris Kam, Sunhi Keller, Dominique Cimina, John Adamo, Catherine O'Mara, Maria Vitale, Sarah Lawrenson, Amy Rockwell, and more—this book would not exist without you. Thank you.

Faye Bender, thank you for being a steadfast, whip-smart champion who never sacrifices kindness. What a joy to have you as an agent.

Thank you to the students at Wing Luke, Sanislo, MLK Jr., Orca, Olympic View, Viewlands, James Baldwin, and Sand Point elementary schools for helping me choose my title. Did I get it right? Let me know.

To Cornelia Li, thank you for this beautiful cover.

All my gratitude to indie booksellers, with special love to PNW indies, and extra special love to Third Place Books.

I am indebted, as always, to the books I read for research: *The Hidden Life of Trees* by Peter Wohlleben; *The Light Eaters* by Zoë Schlanger; *Finding the Mother Tree* by Suzanne Simard; *Indians, Fire, and the Land in the Pacific Northwest* by Robert Boyd; *Fire Weather* by John Vaillant; *Native Seattle* by Coll Thrush; *The Good Rain* by Timothy Egan; *The Forging of a Black Community* by Quintard Taylor; and *Seattle from the Margins* by Megan Asaka.

Speaking of research, I owe a huge thank-you to Kristina